DEITIES

—and—

DUMBASSES

A Collection of Short Stories

by Isaac Nielson

Published by IngramSpark

This is a work of fiction. Names, characters, places, and incidents either are the product of the author's imagination or are used fictitiously. Any resemblance to actual persons, living or dead, events or locales is entirely coincidental.

Cover design by Isaac Nielson
Interior page design and editing by Zach Batt

ISBN: 979-8-9869548-6-8 (ebook)
ISBN: 979-8-9869548-9-9 (print)

Printed in the United States of America.

For Bruce Campbell, John Carpenter, and Kurt Russell. If only you three had collaborated on a better film than Escape from L.A.

Actually for Grant, also known as "The Gator"

CONTENTS

THE FRESH BASTARDS: A TRAGEDY

The bassist, bearded and in all black, followed his bandmates out of their tour bus—steps made heavy by the equipment he carried.

"Why are we doing this again?" he whined.

"James, please listen this time," the portly manager said. "This is The Final Frontier, it's like 'Battle of the Bands' for big boys."

"But we could play a couple shows in Houston and make more money with less hassle!"

The drummer, Chett, turned and clasped James on the shoulder. "You'll be ridin' this tour bus around Houston the rest of your life like that. This is about more than money."

"Fame! It's about fame, baby!" cried the exceptionally thin and gaudy singer.

"You are too vain, Adam my boy," the guitarist, less thin yet equally gaudy, said eloquently as he leaned an arm on his guitar case. "Tonight is, quite simply, for getting high as a fuckin' weather balloon and playing some rock 'n' roll."

The band nodded in agreement, standing in a circle outside of the dingy venue. Before they could get too out of hand with their fantasies, the manager stepped in.

"Will you fucks just get inside and start warming up? We're on in three hours. And Danny," he called, pointing a meaty finger at the guitarist, "don't start that junkie shit. If you dumbasses get too stoned to play, I'll clean your clocks like a sexy French maid!"

"Is that bad?" James whispered to Chett, who murmured affirmatively.

At that moment, a beat-up old sedan slid around the street corner and charged toward the group. When it was dangerously close, the tires squealed and the car turned to the side, stopping just an arm's length from disaster. The doors flew open, and four messy-looking young men tumbled out.

"Coach! Yo, Coach!" one of them yelled, the four reconvening in front of the band after gathering the remaining instruments and supplies from their car.

"You're late, and I'm not your coach," replied the manager.

"Sorry man, we were twistin' and turnin'

y'know?"

"Shut up. No more talking. Everyone go inside right now."

Not wanting to upset the manager any further, the band and their crew shuffled into the building. On the outside, it appeared a dull piece of oversized industry. However, the interior presented a series of corridors surrounding a wide-open area, dotted with ladders and levers, and prematurely cut off by a closed red curtain. It was a locale known as Pandemonium, avoided by locals for the rumors of strange influence and demonic possession felt by those who ventured inside. The owner dismissed these claims until he realized that many of the bands he hosted happened to share an audience with the spectacle of the supernatural. Thereafter, lines like "Prepare for a terrifying night of haunted hellraising!" and "I survived Pandemonium!" were integral parts of all related marketing and merchandise.

"Our practice area should be down the hall to the right. Room 23-C, I believe," the manager explained. "There should be a drum set in there for ya, Chett. Get goin' and start jammin', boys. I hear Larry Longrodd and his group of leather freaks are playing tonight, and I refuse to let those glittered-up perverts beat us out."

Ignoring most of his manager's words, Danny handed his guitar to one of the roadies, whispering, "Take this and go on ahead. Papa needs a little pick-me-up before the show, and everyone knows Longrodd has the good shit."

Danny then ran off in the opposite direction of the practice area and, without delay, the band took advantage of the situation.

"I need to find a nice cold place to prepare my body for the stage," claimed Adam, wandering away.

"Damn it, boys, do you really have to do this every time we're doing something important? Get back here!"

The manager knew his words had no effect, but he had to do what he could. He turned to James and Chett with a sigh, saying, "At least you two are still here. A couple of the roadies can fill in for Danny and Adam, go practice with them before my bullshit reactor has a fucking meltdown."

"Actually, I wanna get kinda weird with it tonight," said James, handing off his bass to the nearest man. "I wanna get up on the catwalks of this place and watch the other bands perform like I'm God or Zeus or whatever. I'll be back a good thirty minutes before showtime. That's as much as we really use for practicing anyway. See ya!"

"No, no, no! Fuck! I'm gonna lose my retirement plan if we don't do something here. Chett, listen up."

"Anything you need, man," the drummer replied. "I don't wanna bomb a show this big."

"I need you to get those idiots into the practice room ASAP. Start with Danny so he doesn't get too high to play. Adam and James will be easier to corral once he's back on task. I'm gonna go pop some pills in the practice room—I feel an aneurysm coming."

With that, Chett bolted after Danny, hoping to find someone along the way who could point him to the Longrodd & The Likkerz practice room. He was so dedicated to chasing Danny that he ran right past James, who was chatting with a stagehand he had stalked from upstage. The young woman laughed and held his hand as she led him along, excitedly describing the wonders of the catwalk.

Danny exhaled a thick cloud of smoke as these events took place. His dedication to his mission had allowed him to find the Longrodd room almost immediately, and the band was more than happy to let him in when he suavely waved his hand and said, "'Sup?" Surrounded by Longrodd's band and groupies, all wearing leather and ten-gallon hats encrusted with fake diamonds, he wanted nothing more than to live in that hazy moment and get as intoxicated as possible before he took the stage. This daydream ended when three loud bangs came from the door.

"Someone answer that," said the man of imposing build in the corner of the room. "It might be an angel."

"Anything for you, Larry," purred one of the groupies, walking to the door and opening it just enough to see outside.

"Is Danny in there?" Chett nearly yelled.

"Is Danny in here?" the groupie repeated to the room behind her.

"Danny, are you in here?" questioned Longrodd with a chuckle.

In a low, raspy voice Danny moaned, "No..." causing the room to fill with cackles and coughs.

"Hey! Either boot him out or let me in. We don't have time for this," Chett barked.

"This guy doesn't sound very cool," Longrodd said, leaning toward Danny. "You know him, right? Is he cool?"

Danny thought for a moment, then sparked his lighter, "Nope. Fuck him."

The door slammed and locked in Chett's face, which was shouting and flinging saliva. He hit the door a few more times, then stomped away in hopeless rage. He would have to try again later.

Longrodd rolled a hundred-dollar bill into a tube shape, "What was that guy's deal?"

"He's in this band called The Fresh Bastards," Danny explained. "Also, I'm in that band."

"No way, dude! You're in a band? Me too!"

"I know, Larry."

Chett returned to the manager, who was now in the practice room watching the roadies perform a mock concert. His face was the very image of anger. The drummer felt like he would rather try to do the whole show himself than face the manager at that moment, but he knew what had to be done. As he approached, the manager suddenly turned to him with a frantic eye.

"Oh, thank God. I assume Danny is on his way? We found Adam in the freezer near the back, but that little chickenshit says he won't come out 'til the whole band's here. You got Danny, right?"

"Uh, not exactly. They locked me out."

"Chett," said the manager, voice gradually raising, "what the fuck are you doing? Lemme tell you somethin' they should have told us ten fuckin' days ago: our time slot got moved up. We're on before Longrodd, now. We barely have time to assemble the band, let alone practice. So please, get those motherfuckers in this room immediately.

See if you can find James quickly and, if not, go grab Adam—you can wrastle him out of there no problem, I'm sure. Go on, get goin'!"

  Chett left the room in a hurry, then paused to take in the manager's words. It was difficult to work with a man who would rather talk at you than with you, but Chett respected him enough to put up with it. He had planned to become a manager himself after retiring from the stage, and this was his opportunity to make connections while learning from "one of the best in the business" as he stated in his newspaper ad.

  High above the stage, upon a metal walkway, James watched a small and insignificant Chett dart through the backstage halls. Everything was so tiny from where he was. He felt like a king. James was never one to play the leader, but he couldn't resist pulling imaginary strings on the little people below him, wicked smile forming on his face. That was when all of the main lights went out at once, burying him in darkness. Startled, he jumped a bit. The massive curtain squeaked open.

  "Don't be afraid, the show's starting," said the stagehand in a low voice.

  "Oh. Uh, can we be up here during the show?" he hurriedly asked, attempting to hide the fact that he had forgotten she was beside him.

"We can do whatever we want up here," she breathed, placing a hand on his shoulder. "You saw it, didn't you? How pitiful they are? How meaningless they become from this height? The catwalk makes us strong. It puts us above the stage lights. It puts us above the show."

"I can kind of understand that, I guess. When I was watching them run around below me I felt like—"

"Like a king?" She gave a throaty laugh, "Yes, you can be a king. You'll be my little king, and, if anyone gets in our way..." she directed his gaze with a gentle hand.

His eyes somewhat adjusting to the darkness, James could discern faint figures floating in the air. They were each quite large and pale white—an army of bloated specters. The stage lights turned on, and he felt a chill as he realized that they weren't simply suspended by some magic spell or trickery. Thick ropes led from the tops of the figures to a darkness even higher above, swaying almost imperceptibly from the building's airflow.

"I put those there a few weeks ago," she continued. "My boss was being a real prick, so I strung up all of our sandbags, get it? They'll fall right between the rest of the rigging. Lots of people have been up here since then, but no one has noticed. It's because they don't understand. They aren't worthy of seeing the truth. They're just pawns."

James was so overwhelmed by the situation that he could not help from being swept into it. The stagehand's words comforted him. They made him feel indomitable. The king looked past the stage and into the sea of spectators, transfixed by how condensed and formless they were in the dim distance.

In a frozen room below, Adam was in deep meditation. He was convinced that he performed at his best after reflecting on how beautiful both he and his voice were, and he felt that the audience could tell when he neglected this ritual. He had recently learned that cold temperatures could be good for the skin, so hosting his hype session in the freezer was a natural choice. Unfortunately for him, the roadies wouldn't let him have much peace. Adam was the only band member they could reliably find, so one by one they interrupted his tranquility with their questions.

"Hey man, are we just doing the usual tuning tonight?"

"Do we have any extra microphone cables?"

"Dude, there's a bunch of crazy fans at the backdoor. Some real cute chicks, I'm tellin' ya. Think they could get your autograph?"

"What's scarier, snakes or spiders?"

His frustrations quickly rose to unbearable levels. He would not have those nitwits ruin his focus, especially at such an important show. After sending them away with some choice words, he removed all of his clothing and began to tie it around the handles of the freezer doors. His body was shaking from the cold, but he reasoned that he would get used to it soon enough. He tied his shirt tight, then his pants even tighter, creating a barrier of two powerful knots between him and the outside world. They could still see him through the small windows on the doors, but he didn't have to look at them. With peace restored, Adam returned to his meditation.

"Look at this guy! He's blasted!" Larry Longrodd said, pointing to one of his band members.

"Hey man, fuck off," the musician replied, struggling to speak.

In the Longrodd practice room, the same group of degenerate druggies sat around a man lying on the floor. One of Longrodd's bandmates, he was expected to be able to hold his own when it came to consuming large amounts of drugs. He couldn't, as it turned out, so the rest of the party took it upon themselves to thoroughly berate him for his weakness.

"I thought you were a tough guy, Joe," said another bandmate sarcastically.

"Come on, man, we got a show in a few minutes here," Longrodd added.

"Brothers," spat the fallen man, "I fear that I cannot go on."

"You must. You absolutely must!" cried a groupie. "It cannot end here!"

"If only we had someone to take over his role on guitar," lamented Longrodd.

Danny, at this point nearly as debilitated as the man on the ground, forgot his responsibilities to his own band in the heat of the moment. He stood and announced that he, in fact, played the guitar. The room was so shocked that they ignored the outburst of desperate knocks at the door.

"Do you know all of our songs?"

Danny snorted, "Do you know all of your songs? It's just gonna be power chords and a big dumb solo, right? I can do that. We have our roadies cover for us all the time. Never taught 'em a single lick."

He felt a hand clasp tightly around his ankle. "My son," Joe said, a tear rolling down his face, "avenge me."

"Give me one of those fuckin' sparkly hats,

and you got a deal."

With the sounds of other bands playing and preparing all around him, the manager was losing the little composition he had left. It would be time for the band to play soon, and he knew that there was little he could do besides take some more pills, prepare the instruments, and hope things work out.

"Move all of our shit down next to the stage," he yelled to the roadies. "It's showtime, and the show must go on!"

Four amplifiers, several varieties of guitar, two pedalboards, and enough cables to hook everything up to the house equipment—all hauled down to the side of the stage, ready for action. The roadies were tired, but they weren't done yet. The band still had to appear. Those brave young men felt pride and determination flourish within them as they listened to the manager's heartfelt speech, in which he detailed how important the roadies were to the band, and how they were the only ones who could save this disastrous concert. Of course, none of them remembered much from the speech after about five minutes, but the emotions still lingered. They were ready to do what they had to do.

In all of the darkness and chaos of the live show, the roadies doubted they could find anyone who was roaming around. However, they knew where at least one band member was, so they ran to the walk-in freezer at the back of the venue.

"Try the doors," one of them said.

"He tied 'em shut, remember?" replied another.

"Do it anyway, bang on the windows, I don't know."

The roadies spent the next few minutes taking turns pulling on the doors, slapping the windows, and arguing. Their commotion was so great that the fans at the backdoor heard them, reigniting their passion for trying to get up close and personal with the band. Eventually, one of the roadies determined that their approach wasn't working, so he leaned into the window on the left door to get a look at what was happening inside. He paused, then backed up.

"Oh shit, boys," he gasped. "Adam's fucking dead."

This would ordinarily be taken as a joke, but the dread on his face convinced the other roadies to huddle around the windows and see for themselves. The room appeared to be empty, until their eyes moved down to reveal a nude and unmoving body stretched out toward them. Adam's arms were still held up, his hands frozen to the knots he failed to untie in time. Likewise, his eyes were fixed on his final task, as if he still believed he could escape.

"Oh shit, man! What do we do?" began the babbling between the four roadies.

"I don't know, dude! This has never happened before!"

"Really? I thought we lost band members every other day!"

"Quit fuckin' around, we gotta think of something!"

"What's going on, guys?"

They all turned to see Chett standing in the middle of the hallway. He had a worried expression and was fidgeting impatiently. He tried to come closer, but the roadies advanced first, hoping to stall him until they could come up with some kind of plan.

"Nothin's goin' on, man. We're just tryin' to get Adam out of his icebox."

"Yeah. He, uh, said he won't come out until someone deals with the fans at the backdoor."

Chett scowled, "What the fuck? That asshole knows damn well the show's about to start. I'm just gonna drag him out of there."

"No! I mean, um, nope, you don't wanna do that. We tried that earlier."

"He's got a gun, man. He's totally off the deep end."

"We've just gotta do what he wants, for now."

"Those fans won't leave until someone from the band calms them down. They're crazy, and there's no damn security in this place. Please, man. We need your help."

With the show falling apart around him, Chett saw the light of destiny. He knew at that moment that he was the only one who could save the night. He told the roadies to wait, then marched toward the backdoor. They watched him open the door and step outside but, as the door shut behind him, they heard a chilling scream. Confused and terrified, they retreated back to the stage.

Outside, Chett was dealing with the fans, who all went wild with cheers and shrieks when they saw one of their idols. He tried to explain the situation to them, then to at least calm them down, and finally to just make them go away. None of it worked, and the crowd of drooling devotees became more and more ravenous. They moved closer to Chett; one of them dared to reach out and touch his shoulder. In seconds, their hands were all over him, pulling him in every direction as each fan tried to get the most of The Fresh Bastards that they could. His skin ripped, his organs burst, even his bones were pulled apart. The fanatics howled before scampering away with their prizes. Chett became nothing more than a collection of morbid souvenirs for his most passionate followers.

"What the hell are you doing back here? Where's my fuckin' band?" the manager roared at the roadies.

"We couldn't find anyone," one of them explained.

"Yeah, uh, even Adam's gone. At least, he was when we looked."

"You tellin' me the night's totally fucked?" the manager began to rant, getting louder and more red in the face with each word. "Go ahead, tell me the night's totally fucked. I already know it is. Tell me I worked my fuckin' balls off every day to get these worthless phallus fiddlers in here, and nothin's gonna come of it because every single fucking person involved is shit-for-brains incompetent! Oh yeah, that includes me. I'm the goddamn clown in this circus! Everything I do is a joke, and no one respects me!"

At that moment, the manager's eye was caught by the glint of several sparkling hats as they moved onto the stage. Longrodd & The Likkerz appeared to have not known about the scheduling change, and were now playing in The Fresh Bastards' time slot. Hope welled within him. He saw an opportunity to get his band together while the competition played. Then, he noticed who was playing guitar for Longrodd. He unconsciously reached for his bottle of pills.

"What in the son-of-a-bitch hell-devil fuck is he doing playing for those shitheads? Did he fry his brain for real this time? Fuck!" The manager chewed a couple of pills and swallowed them. "Maybe this is alright. He ain't goin' anywhere, and we can still find everyone else. I can make this work. I can pull this fucking circus together!"

Longrodd & The Lickerz kicked-off their set with a fast-paced tune, rousing the audience to a frenzy. James and the stagehand watched, unseen and unheard by anyone else. Thus far, James had been enjoying his time on the catwalk, watching live performances while the beautiful woman beside him whispered pleasant things in his ear. Her musings gave him a strange feeling at first but, in time, he found himself almost as engaged in her fantasies as she was. He was a king, and the theater his kingdom. Because of this, his happiness rapidly faded, and the stagehand took notice.

"What's wrong, my king?"

"Look at them, that awful band. They have the audacity to pollute my air with their sounds, and the commoners are reveling in it!"

"Oh, enemies in the court?" she said with a

laugh. "I think it's time to use my special weapon."

He imagined destroying them, making his court pure. He grinned, "Excellent idea."

James followed the stagehand to an even darker corner of the catwalk, where a lever with a lock around it sat isolated. She removed the lock and beckoned him closer. His hand was guided to the lever, and wrapped around it tightly. There was a flicker of rational doubt in his mind, but a kiss from the stagehand made it vanish. He pulled the lever and felt more bliss than ever he had in his life. It was him who saved the kingdom from evil. James had confirmed in his mind that he was meant to be king.

"Great job, little king," the stagehand said, grabbing him with both hands and incredible strength. "Now, it's time for you to go, as well."

"What do you mean? I'm your king!" he cried, snapping out of his trance.

"You don't even know my name! You aren't worthy of standing upon the catwalk! You're only another pawn!"

"Hogwash! I bet you don't know my name! I'm the king, damn it! Let go of me!"

"Come on, James, I know everything about you. You married too soon, got divorced, and wound up spiraling down into debauchery. You came up here to see what sort of trouble you could get into, and that has led to your demise. I made you my king but, here, I am still your god."

The stagehand pulled him backward over the railing of the catwalk and slowly past the point of no return.

"I could be worthy of the catwalk if you give me a chance," James pleaded as his upper half dangled over the edge. "Please! Let me rule this kingdom a little longer! Give me a chance!"

"You had plenty of chances. My name is Julia," she said, dragging him fully over the railing and allowing him to fall, shattering the king upon the ground of peasants.

The theater was filled with the sounds of terror. Longrodd & The Likkerz, along with Danny, had been severely crushed and mangled under the sandbags. Spectators scrambled to find the exits, ultimately congesting them to the point of uselessness in their attempt to distance themselves from the blood and bits of gore. The manager was utterly stunned. His chest felt tight, and his entire body trembled. The roadies seemed strangely unaffected, as if already acclimated to an environment of death.

"Well, there goes Longrodd," one roadie sighed.

"What do we do now?" asked another.

"How about you call a fuckin' ambulance!" the manager exclaimed. "I think I'm dyin' here!"

"Honestly, man, that's a pretty insensitive joke considering the situation."

"The only thing we can do is help the audience. They've gotta be traumatized," continued the roadies, ignoring the manager's ongoing wails.

"Boys, I think I get it." The other roadies gathered around him like rallying troops. "It's showtime, right?"

"Right!" the three repeated.

The roadie leading the discourse looked to the manager and winked, "Then the show must go on!"

"Hell yeah!"

"Grab the equipment. We'll plug into whatever is left out there and give those people their money's worth!"

They proceeded onto the stage, continuing to holler and build their own energy. They had surprisingly little trouble setting up, as only a few house speakers had been crushed. Some of the drum set was missing, but the roadie playing it said he could make it work, pushing a corpse out of his way as he spoke. To their side, the manager passed away, using his last breath to string together every curse he knew into a masterstroke insult directed at the roadies.

With an audience of swarming paramedics, police, and terrified attendees, the roadies started to play. Having no plan or set list, they were disjointed at first, and felt a little thankful for all of the noise covering up their mistakes. Regardless, they kept playing, and their discordant jam morphed into a real song, which one of the roadies managed to improvise a few lyrics over. Some of the audience members stopped to listen, causing even more problems for those trying to evacuate. The song ended in a spectacular explosion of instrumentation, with spontaneously synchronized solos and a massive wall of sound to wash it all away. The roadies gathered close once more.

"That was fuckin' awesome!"

"Fuck yes, dude! That was rock 'n' roll!"

"But—hey, boys, what do we do now?"

"Well, we didn't get booed."

The four musicians nodded, returning to their positions on stage.

GLASS CASTLES

Dragging his trashcan to the curb, Mike smiled in the lonely night. He didn't often smile, nor did he particularly enjoy taking out the trash, but he felt at peace with his tiny world at the end of 33rd Street. Having just cleaned and organized his home, the high of total sovereignty was still strong and pulsating. This supreme ecstasy continued until, disastrously, Mike made the mistake of looking toward his neighbor's house.

To an outside observer, it would seem a mirror image—trashcan sitting in the proper place for morning collection—but Mike knew better. He trampled the grass that connected their driveways with a nervous speed, hands nearly shaking as he threw open the lid. The buzz of delight turned to boiling rage; his suspicions were confirmed.

"Why the fuck don't you bag your trash?" Mike snarled through gritted teeth, slamming the can closed. He grabbed it by the handle and began to pull it back to the house, continuing to rant as he set the stage for his perceived revenge.

"All it takes is a strong gust of wind—then boom! Trash all over the damn place, and we both know your lazy ass won't clean it up. Shit, forget wind, a raccoon will do it just for fun!"

Mike rammed the trashcan down where it usually sat, next to his neighbor's garage door.

"Are you having fun?" he yelled as he gave the can a solid string of kicks. "Huh? Are you?"

Having let off some steam, Mike stomped back to his house, shoved shut and locked the door behind him, then promptly went to bed.

The next day, Mike awoke around noon. He had that day off from work, so there was no rush to regain consciousness. Lazily strolling out to collect his mail, he saw his most loathed neighbor loitering in the road. The man's name was Lion, and his carefree attitude was certainly fitting for the head of a pride. With a smug step, Mike approached.

"How ya doin', bud?" he called in a casual tone.

"Splendid, my main man Mike," came the reply. "Resplendent, in fact."

"Didn't see your can out last night. Did you miss trash day?"

"Almost! Luckily, the thunderstorm woke me up in the night. Couldn't get back to sleep, but I did get my trash out bright and early," Lion said, punctuating his statement with an ear-to-ear smile. Mike hurried to find something to say before his scowl became too obvious.

"And, uh, you bagged it this time, right?" he questioned in a jolly tone.

"Ah, y'know, I forgot again. But it turned out okay."

"Funny how things work out," Mike mumbled.

"For sure. Sometimes the universe just puts you where you need to be," Lion sang. "Oh! Speaking of which, I think Bill's kid wanted to play catch, so I'm gonna head over there now. Talk to you later, buddy."

"Yeah, talk to you later, catch you later, see you later, whatever," Mike rambled as he turned and walked away.

A few minutes later, Lion arrived at Bill's house, waiting only a short moment after knocking on the front door before it opened, unveiling the man himself.

"Lion! How's it goin', brother?" Bill nearly shouted. "Timmy's grounded right now 'cuz he lost his bike—fuckin' fool—but ya'll can play for a bit.

He needs the exercise."

Lion leaned in close and spoke with a hushed voice, "Actually, could I talk to you real quick?"

"Uh, yeah man, sure. What's up?"

"I was just talking to Mike, and I think he's really upset about something."

"Again? You sure it ain't that he don't like you?"

"No no no, this time it's different." Lion moved even closer. "You didn't hear it from me, but I think he's gonna hurt himself, or someone else."

"Aw hell," said Bill with gravity. "Can't have that. Tell ya what, we'll play ball with Timmy, and I'll send my wife over to check on him."

"You'd do that?" Lion replied with hope.

"No problem." Bill turned around and bellowed into his house, "Martha! Where you at, woman?"

"Whaddya want?" she bellowed back as she walked into view of the men. When she saw Lion she blushed in embarrassment, and her voice lowered with her head, "Oh, hi, Lion."

"Mike's goin' a little crazy," Bill said without skipping a beat. "Think you could go over and talk to him?"

"Of course. I love babysitting fully grown

men."

"You're so nice," Lion said to the air around him.

As Bill was wrangling Timmy out of his room, Mike was finishing his sixth beer. Mike believed that time without work was best spent drunk, and he practiced what he preached. A rather biased newscaster was frantically explaining how unbiased they were on the television in front of him when the sound of a doorbell echoed through the home. Mike groaned, lurching out of his chair before shuffling to the door. He paused for a moment, hoping whoever it was would go away, but ultimately greeted his guest as the doorbell cried out once more.

"Afternoon, Martha," he said without glee.

"Hi, Mike," she spoke in a drawn-out, concerned tone. "How are you doing? Is everything okay?"

"Did Lion send you?"

"You didn't hear it from me."

Mike sighed, "You want a beer?"

"Please," she replied with relief, following him into his home.

Both parties now seated in front of Mike's television, they cracked their cans of liquid relaxation and began their discourse.

"So, there's nothing going on?" Martha inquired.

"Not with me, but that Lion guy's a fuckin' nut," Mike clarified.

"I've come to learn that over the years. He seems kind of sneaky."

"My son's a fag, y'know?" Mike went to sip his beer, then withdrew. "Gay, sorry. Got nothin' against the gays, I just wish the little bastard would come out and tell me like a man. Anyway, I'm not one to point fingers, but he used to hang out with that weirdo a lot before he moved away."

"What are you saying?" Martha asked. "What are you getting at?"

"Like I said, I'm not one to point fingers. I just noticed an effect and I'm looking for a cause. He hangs out with your kid a lot now. I'm curious to see how young Tim turns out."

Martha wanted to curse at him, but a part of her mind understood his position. Bill had been saying similar things ever since Mike's son went off to college, claiming he only let Timmy play with Lion because the boy whined too much otherwise. She didn't agree with their blatant bigotry, but could not deny the odd feeling she often experienced when watching the perpetually single and childless Lion entertain the neighborhood kids without supervision. She guzzled down her beer in a single pull.

"Mike, I don't like you," she began.

"I can respect that," Mike interrupted.

"Right. As I was saying, I don't like you, but I do love my son, and I agree that Lion gives off a strange vibe sometimes. That's why Bill is always there when Timmy plays with him."

"I wouldn't even let that happen, now that I know how devious that creep can be. Y'know, I bought the house at the end of the street so I'd only have one neighbor to worry about, but he's been trouble enough for a whole damn apartment complex! Fucker doesn't even bag his trash."

"Really? What if a raccoon got in it, or the wind blew it over?"

"That's what I've been saying!" Mike blurted loudly. "You gotta watch out for that guy."

"For sure." Martha stood to make her exit. "I oughta get back to Bill now. Thanks for the beer, and I'm glad everything's okay with you."

"One more thing," Mike said with slightly slurred speech. "Why can I call someone from England an Englishman, but I can't call a Chinaman a Chinaman?"

"Goodbye, Mike."

The rest of the day went relatively without

incident. Martha, upon returning home and seeing Bill, Lion, and Timmy playing a harmless game of catch, decided to keep her conversation with Mike to herself. However, Lion went home shortly after noticing her gaze, and she could not help but think that he saw some disdain in her eyes.

The sun rose on the next morning, and Mike followed it with a somewhat-hungover sluggishness. He made a mental note to pace himself on nights before work, stowing it away with hundreds of identical notes he had made in the past. Having donned his office-approved outfit, he tied his corporate leash in a Windsor knot and headed to his garage. There, he shambled into his sedan, started the engine, and began another nine-hour journey to and from what he considered contemporary serfdom.

Mike didn't exactly hate his job. It was easy and garnered decent pay. However, years of working under multiple bosses, being chewed-out multiple times for minute errors, and never seeing any tangible results from these efforts had worn him down to a tired nub. The walls of his cubicle became the constricting stomach of a predator which had swallowed him whole, and he could feel himself slowly dissolving in the digestive acids.

This day was no different, and Mike

returned to his neighborhood exhausted. Pulling into his driveway, he glanced over at Lion's house, and all rational thought crumbled under the weight of newfound fury. It wasn't that anything was wrong, but rather that something could go wrong. Why should he bother waiting for Lion's next stunt, when he had already dealt with them for years? Colors swirled and shifted to a deep murky red as 33rd Street warped into a wicked abomination of chaotic possibilities. The time of underhanded tactics had ended. Mike saw no other option but to seize dominion by force.

Lion's front door erupted with sound, nearly succumbing to the repeated assault of Mike's fist. Fortunately for that slab of wood, Mike soon realized that Lion was likely somewhere else in the area, as he often wandered around and into other people's business until sunset. Sure enough, Mike found his target at the nearby hill where children would often play. There, Lion was engaged in a game of ball tag with some local kids—those who were not currently grounded for losing their bikes.

Marching with great ferocity, Mike arrived at the base of the hill. Lion, who stood atop the summit, looked down on him and smiled, feigning ignorance in the increasingly heavy atmosphere. The hill shook as if assailed by a terrible disaster as

Mike began to ascend. However, this ascension was brought to an abrupt halt when he met a militia of innocent faces.

"Don't hurt him!" one of the kids cried.

"What?" Mike faltered, taken back by this sudden confrontation.

"Lion said you're a bad man," called another child. "He said you stole Timmy's bike!"

"Mine too!" came the voice of a third.

"You lost yours in the creek, remember?" questioned another.

"Oh, right."

"Get out of my way, you little fucks!" Mike roared, collecting himself.

The kids scattered. One of them dropped the ball they had been playing with, but did not dare retrieve it as it rolled down the hill to where Mike stood. He glanced at the ball and, when he looked back up, Lion was directly in front of him, wielding a gentle smirk.

"Alright you slimy shitsnake, start talkin'," Mike growled.

"I'm sorry, my friend," Lion spoke with an unrelenting calmness. "I was attempting to hasten the destruction of your ego, so that you might be set free."

"You wanna elaborate on that?"

"We don't exist."

"Oh, please!" Mike almost laughed. "Spare me the whole 'nothing is real' spiel, you hippy fuck."

Lion actually did laugh, "There are many things which exist. You and I do not. We are but phantoms.'"

"Okay, idiot. If I don't exist, then how can I do this?" Mike asked, lightly kicking the ball at his foot up the hill.

"You did nothing," Lion responded. Mike looked down to find the ball had rolled back and stopped by his foot once again.

"Oh, fuck off!" he declared, this time striking the ball so hard it went over the hill and disappeared. "I have a kid! I have a job! You have nothing! You're the one who doesn't exist, so don't rope me in with you!"

"I think we should go our separate ways and cool off for a bit."

"That's the first smart thing I've ever heard you say. You just saved yourself from a serious ass beating."

"See you later, Mike," Lion said as he made a lackadaisical exit.

"Bye-bye!" Mike hollered after him, still quite impassioned. "I'm gonna go drink beer!

Lots of beer! And if I see you, I'm gonna rip your goddamn cock in half!"

Without looking, Lion waved to Mike with the back of his hand, silently reiterating his parting words. Mike remained at the base of the hill for a while longer, grumbling and pacing around in circles. Eventually, when dusk had solidified its presence, his front door slammed and his beers cracked—the signal that their enraged master had returned.

While Mike downed can after can, he reflected on his actions. He was certain that Lion needed a good thrashing, but wondered if it was his place to provide it. They would still be neighbors, and tensions probably wouldn't decrease. Perhaps a different strategy would yield better results, he reasoned. Mike released a powerful belch as he schemed to befriend Lion and change him through suggestion. Pondering the fine details of this, a knock upon his door disclosed the object of his new plan.

"Please don't rip my cock in half, man," Lion besought Mike as he opened the door. "I wanted to tell you that I'm sorry—actually sorry— for messing with you."

"I ain't gonna touch your dick, bud. I was just angry," Mike assured him.

"Could we try to put this all behind us?"

Mike's heart skipped. "You know what, why not? Come on in and have a beer."

"No. I'm all right for tonight, thanks," Lion said quickly, eyes wide.

"Didn't expect me to want to cooperate, did you?"

"You got me," Lion chuckled, his body rotating toward his own home. "I'm actually cooking some stuff right now, so I can't hang out. Maybe tomorrow we'll plan something."

"Yeah, we can do that. Have a good night, man."

Mike closed the front door, and immediately ran to the nearest window. The fires of bestial animosity reignited in his gut, burning stronger than ever. He watched Lion reach his house, look behind him, and enter with a swift step. At that moment, Mike resolved to follow him—having lost all doubt that his neighbor was engaged in nefarious obscurities. Everyone on 33rd Street knew that Lion never cooked.

For better or worse, Mike came to find that Lion had left the front door unlocked. The dimly lit night gave way to awful darkness as Mike slipped through, closing the door quietly behind him. Faced with total blindness, he stood unmoving until his eyes adjusted, and almost took flight when they did.

The room before him, faintly visible by a distant radiation, was a villainous carnival of things frivolously removed from being orderly—as if made unkempt by a deliberate hand and a determination to spite his very being. A box of juvenile toys sat overflowing in the corner, adorning the floor with the shapes of dolls and pinwheels. The walls, which were otherwise pristine, displayed intermittent deep lacerations, decorated with small splatters of dark. There was a ceiling fan, but one of the blades was bent upward to the extent of touching the plaster, rendering the whole contraption useless. Even the silence of this scene was at once undone by the muffled sounds of screaming, and metal clashing against metal.

Steeling himself, Mike crept toward the light with caution. A sense of duty shut out all fear. Whatever heinous display awaited him, he knew that he would never again feel at peace if he retreated now. His guiding star revealed itself to be a crack under a door in the kitchen—an area that held no evidence of recent culinary activity. Opening that door exposed a long and unfinished set of stairs, leading deep beneath the safe surface of Earth. This passage was adorned with panels of soundproofing and, without their protection, the shrieks and clangs intensified immensely. Mike descended as the voice became more distinct and clear.

"Fucking cunts! Piece-of-shit dickhead jerks! You're all worthless filth!" it announced shrilly.

Reaching the bottom of the staircase, Mike saw at last the mastermind of this nightmare. Lion was hunched over in the concrete basement, back turned as he slammed an iron pipe continuously against a pile of twisted spokes and handlebars. The missing bicycles of neighborhood children bowed and broke apart under his wrath.

"Holy shit," Mike said, causing the banging to come to a sudden stop.

"Oh, Mike!" Lion exclaimed, spinning to face the trespasser. "Didn't see ya there, buddy! How ya doin'? We still plannin' for tomorrow?"

A familiar glint caught Mike's eye, and he recognized the body of the bike he bought for his son long ago. "I knew that little fucker didn't lose it! I raised him too smart for that! Shoulda just told me, ya damn freak."

"This, um, this isn't what it looks like. I found these bikes! I'm just fixing them up before I return them; don't get the wrong idea."

"This is sad, man—even for you," Mike's

words were dripping with disappointment.

"What do you mean 'even for me'?" Lion replied, his voice again filling with anger. "Sad? You don't get to decide that! You're just an alcoholic nut with anger problems! This street would be a cesspool without me! I pull the strings! I am your God!"

"All these years, and we never noticed you were up to some crazy shit. I mean, I figured you were doin' something, but this is bad comedy."

"You never noticed 'cuz you're a moron!" Lion spewed as he battered another bicycle for emphasis. "At least I vent my anger privately; you're a menace in comparison! The kids are scared of you, but they trust me—see? I deserve this respite! This is a hero's reward!"

"Yeah, I'm goin' home. This is stupid. See ya tomorrow."

Lion cackled maniacally, "You won't be going home, peon! Guess what? I've concluded that you have no place in my world! I'm gonna eat your flesh, crush your bones, and tell your son you killed yourself because you knew how fucking worthless your life was! No one is going to bother looking for you, because everyone thinks you're a selfish asshole! Lay down and die, miserable dog!"

Lion charged at Mike—holding the pipe

high above his head. Mike scrambled up the stairs, but Lion followed close behind. A hand shot out and grabbed Mike's ankle, causing him to fall and strike his chest on the edge of the hardwood. Lion crashed the iron into the side of Mike's knee, rendering it useless. He raised his weapon once more, but Mike's other leg shot out automatically, striking Lion in the chin with a forceful heel. The man of the house tumbled backward; the intruder scurried up and away on three limbs. Mike heard the slap of Lion's skull against the ground as he made his escape.

For a brief moment, he hesitated at the entrance of the appalling lair. Then, gathering his available saliva at the edge of his mouth, he spat upon the floor before continuing onward. When Mike returned to the comfort of his abode, he didn't even bother to lock the door as he retired to bed. Lion had felt the sting of defeat and the humiliation of his disguise's thorough death. Mike knew that he would not henceforth endeavor to show himself, even if it would be to avenge his fallen status. They were neighbors, at any rate.

Managing a much-needed rest, Mike again awoke at noon. He hardly even cared that he was late for work. Uncovering the mysteries of the previous night had given him a strange satisfaction, and the world felt bright and weightless. He encountered some trouble in clothing himself with his injuries, but nonetheless slipped on some garments and hobbled outside. There, he beheld Lion's garage and front door wide open, with a sign in the lawn reading "FOR SALE." Mike's trashcan had been flipped upside down over a nearby storm drain. On the hill in the distance, there was a collection of jumbled tires and aluminum, glistening in the sunlight.

KONBINI COWBOY

I walked into Joe's Convenience with a burning hunger in my gut. They had plenty of pizza on the rack, but Joe couldn't make a pizza to save his life—or his business. At Joe's, it was all about the hot dogs. I turned down the aisle to find that they had two left. Perfect.

After the dogs were in buns and covered in condiments, I headed straight for the cashier. Three young burnouts were standing in line, holding bags of chips and some of that infamous pizza. Amateurs. A place like Joe's is only convenient if you know how to play the game.

"Must be their first time here," I said to the cashier as I slapped down a couple of bucks. She laughed but also gave me a funny look. Probably wasn't used to hearing a non-employee discussing insider knowledge. Nice gal, nonetheless.

I saw those same burnouts sitting in

the parking lot, eating their pizza. They looked disappointed. A lesson had been learned that day. I took a bite of one of my hot dogs as I passed. No sympathy. It was delicious, and I had taken their entire stock. To the victor go the spoils, and I never lose. Not when it comes to convenience stores.

Well, that isn't entirely true. I lost once, and that opened my eyes. Back then, I didn't know shit about convenience. I used to think stores like that were useless, only selling inferior versions of things you could find elsewhere. We were all dumb kids once, after all.

It was at a store called Lawman's Station— brightly lit little joint with shelves that always seemed a bit too tall. I don't like shopping there anymore but, again, I didn't know any better at the time. Anyway, I wandered in all wide eyed, seeing the abundant varieties of food and household items they put out for sale. I'd been to a convenience store before, but never one that sold freshly-made meals. It had totally caught me off-guard.

I stood in front of those clear plastic boxes for a while, examining my options. They had chicken, mashed potatoes, steak—you name it. I almost asked the cashier if there was a restaurant in the back. That's when a lean fella with a broad-brimmed hat walked by, carrying a bag of beef jerky and a bottle of water.

"You don't want any of that," he said. "Not unless you want to be stuck on the toilet for the rest of the day."

I didn't get the chance to reply. When I turned around, he was already paying for his items and making idle chit-chat with the employees. At first, I wasn't even sure if he had said that to me or not. He did everything so quickly and smoothly that it was like he was never there. I should have followed his advice. I should have followed him. I should have just swallowed my pride, grabbed the nearest bag of chips off the shelf, and asked him to teach me his ways. Again, I didn't know shit back then.

They didn't write the prices on the boxed meals, and I found out why when I took one to the cash register. They really must have had a restaurant in the back, because I seemed to be paying the wages of multiple cooks. Regardless, I had already bought the meal—a chicken breast with a pile of corn on the side—so I was determined to enjoy it.

Say what you may about my common sense back then, I at least had the decency to heat the thing up first. There was a good amount of steam coming from it when I took the lid off, and it had an acceptable smell. Taste was another story.

Maybe the plastic container rubbed off on the food, or maybe they found a way to make meals out of recycled paper. Either way, I certainly wasn't tasting chicken, and the corn wasn't much better. I should have tossed it, but I didn't want to waste my money, even though anyone with half a brain knows I already had.

That was one of the worst meals of my life, and the man's advice turned out to be downright prophetic. Probably went through two rolls of toilet paper that day alone, and another one the next morning. I still don't know what the hell they put in that food, but I'd bet it'd have qualified as an agent of biological warfare. Some serious shit, no pun intended.

I never saw that man again, but I understood him better every day. There was something about the way he operated in that store. You might have thought he owned the place if he wasn't purchasing from them. You can't get that kind of style at a supermarket or a proper restaurant. Too bloated, and usually packed with idiots. The slim-slick efficiency of convenience stores revealed itself to me at that time, and they became my usual haunts.

It was a slow process to become a master. I made a few more bad purchases, though none worse than the one at Lawman's Station. A bag of half-crushed chips, a watery fountain soda, and the pizza at Joe's Convenience were among the worst offenders in my rogues' gallery. Watching other people make mistakes allowed me to avoid them. I gained slivers of knowledge each and every time I saw a grimacing face with a mouthful of whatever awful thing they had the misfortune of buying. They were sinking, I was rising to the top.

Of course, food ain't the only thing at a convenience store. When it rained, I knew I could stop by Frank's Necessities for an umbrella. One Stop Palace had the cheapest sunglasses to buy once things cleared up. In the winter, they all sold big metal snow shovels—most of them overpriced. I didn't own a car, but I still made sure to familiarize myself with all the different types of oil and windshield wipers. Chuck's Checkout was the cheapest place for auto supplies, but they were low quality. The real best bang for your buck was Blacktop Convenience, which you'd think would be obvious, but their stock was always full when I checked.

Things change over time, though. Prices shift, and competition swaps around. When I started tracking this, I'd go all giddy imagining who might take the throne for cheapest air freshener or best box of nachos next. It became my life. It gave me life.

Before long, there wasn't a doubt in my mind that I was better at getting the most out of those stores than just about anyone. The art of convenience shopping was both my nature and my conduct.

After finishing the second hot dog, I took a stroll to the local park. Can't spend your whole day in the convenience store, otherwise it didn't do its job properly. I've never been a particularly busy man, but I like to pretend that I am for a few hours a day—always have. There's a certain authority in having somewhere else to be. People get out of your way, and you're free to hurl profanities if they don't. Sometimes I'll say I have a meeting to get to, or I gotta pick up my kids from school. Any miniscule thing to give a sense of urgency, shortly before returning to going about my day in my usual lazy wont. Nowadays I like to sit by the lake and stare at the water but, at this time, I was into the park.

As much as I used to watch people in the convenience stores, I hated and still hate watching them anywhere else. I know there are plenty of folks who enjoy seeing what someone does when they think no one is looking, especially in a public place, but that has never interested me. I don't care about people I haven't met. They hold no value for me. If they strike up a conversation, then we've met and I can start putting in more effort. Otherwise, unless I see them trying out a new item at the convenience store, they might as well not exist.

When I sat in the park, I would watch the grass blow in the wind. Sometimes I'd slowly trace the pattern upward, through the grass and into the air, trying to watch the wind itself. It felt like I almost could catch a glimpse of it, but I never did. That day was no different, and the time I spent waiting for those hot dogs to digest was par for the course.

Having had enough of nature, I wandered back to the industrialized world. I didn't have a goal in mind, but I knew that I'd probably have to use the bathroom soon. There were portable toilets near the park, but you'd have to be idiotic or uninformed to use one of those. Absolutely no sense in cramming yourself into a nasty plastic box when you could easily walk a short distance farther and use a full-sized bathroom. That's the game of convenience.

Nature called, and I directed myself toward the nearest convenience store—a pretty big and fancy place named ConviCorral. A woman was sitting in her car in the handicapped parking space, no indication of disability, eating a soggy-looking taco and frowning at it. Novices should just stick to chips, I thought as I entered the building. There were four rows of shelves inside, and a selection of fresh food on the far wall. Their pizza was slightly better than Joe's, but not by much. That said, it was definitely better than the tacos, and they put out entire pizzas at once instead of just slices. They left a triangular pizza spatula on the counter, and sometimes people would have to use it to separate the slices when they weren't cut well enough. That wasn't my concern at this time, though.

I nodded to the cashier as I entered, making it clear that I was friendly but not too talkative. I then headed straight for the back of the store, where their bathrooms were located. The nice thing about this store was that the bathrooms were for single occupants only, meaning they could be locked for extra privacy and security. I've never been shy or anything like that, but I don't see much point in doing your business so close to someone else. Doesn't feel right. Too animalistic.

I locked the door behind me and got to work. The inexperienced make many mistakes here because, as nice as having an easily accessible bathroom is, the room and toilet are often absolutely filthy. There's no reason to get an illness from the last slob that blasted his germs all over the place, or from some kind of built-up gunk on the surface that can't even be seen. The method is simple. Go into the bathroom, lock the door, and inspect the situation. If that toilet isn't certified and proven one hundred percent spotless clean, fix it up as best you can with the toilet paper and soap. Even if it is spotless, be sure to remove the outer layer of toilet paper that's in the open air, as it's likely covered in particles that shot out the last time the toilet flushed. Do the same thing with the paper towels if they've got them. After that, wash your hands thoroughly, like a doctor. Now you're ready.

Having performed this procedure, my bathroom experience that day was perfectly pleasant. Since the toilet was in its own stall, I was able to push the flush lever with my foot and sidestep out of the stall door before the flushing began, preventing a majority of the airborne particles from touching me. As I washed my hands for the second time, I heard a man shouting in another part of the building, his voice softened by the walls. I had purchased from this cashier before, so I knew he wasn't hard of hearing. The shouting didn't sound like someone simply unaware of their own volume. No combination of explanations in everyday life matched what I was experiencing. Something was wrong.

I put my entire hand over the locking

mechanism to muffle it—germs be damned. I then turned the knob completely so the hardware wouldn't scrape, and pushed the door open just far enough to take a look outside. As I had suspected, this was no ordinary situation.

Average-sized guy with gelled hair, baggy sweat-stained shirt. He had a pistol pointed right at the cashier's face, finger on the trigger. The cashier was doing his best to comply, but he was so nervous that he kept pressing the wrong button on the register, much to the robber's dismay. I probably wouldn't have involved myself, but there was only one exit to the store and I had already done what I needed to do. I wanted to head out, preferably without becoming a hostage or a corpse, and preferably soon. The man might have had a gun, but the way he held it told me he hadn't a clue what he was doing. I didn't know anything about firearms back then, and I still don't, but it didn't look like he had any respect for the thing. One twitch of his finger could have ended the cashier's life, yet he carried himself with the body language of a child throwing a tantrum. Amateur.

I crouched down low and walked out of the bathroom, making sure to keep the doorknob turned as the door closed so it wouldn't make any noise. I knew it was a tricky spot to be in; I'd have nowhere to run if he spotted me. Not only that, but I don't think I would have complied with whatever that hoodlum told me to do, so I'd have probably ended up dead as disco.

I can't say I've ever cared a whole lot for my own life. I enjoy living, I don't want to die, but I don't have much of a track record to uphold. Before I found my calling, I was lower than those kids out in Joe's parking lot. Pops kicked me out when I was sixteen; said I was getting too big to fit in his house. Ma told me it was because he knew he couldn't beat me if I got ornery. He was scared, that's all. What a fuckin' joke.

I lost five teeth earning my place with some street kids my age. I could take 'em one-on-one, but that's why they'd gang up on me. Didn't hurt much, but I wasn't a fan of the blood in my mouth. After I broke a couple of their bones, they stopped messing with me and started trying to be friends. I'd hang out with them, but it never felt like we were all that close. I didn't want them to drag me down, and they weren't willing to climb their way up.

Still, there was one advantage to my short-term friendships. Illegal transactions, theft, and a few muggings ended up netting them a fair horde of cash. Their ragtag gang was known in the area for its escapades, but they somehow avoided getting caught for what felt like far too long. I never got my hands dirty; my job was higher up in the chain. I took the money we didn't need for food and put it into stocks—fake identity being the only crime tied to my face. It didn't do much for us at first, but it snowballed over time. I had an eye for stocks, or I just kept getting lucky. Either way, the night when I finally left that group, nabbing all the hard cash they had on my way out, I had a nice enough portfolio to keep myself afloat without really doing much work. Convenient.

It wasn't like I had a place to go or something to do, I just knew I was better alone. A week later when three of them got shot and the rest were arrested, I felt content with my decision. I bought eight copies of that newspaper, just to make sure the pictures weren't the result of a rare printing error. I almost felt bad for leaving them high and dry like that, but they never quite managed to gain my respect beforehand. They were novices with no intention of improving.

Life was fairly empty for a while after that. Sometimes I'd do odd jobs just for fun. The stocks never paid enough to get a house or anything nice, but I eventually landed myself a shoddy small apartment with complimentary six-legged roommates. If only I knew about the deals on roach killer that Chuck's Checkout had at the end of certain months. Like I said, we were all dumb kids once.

I wormed my way around to the far aisle, taking care not to touch anything or make too heavy of a step. The funny thing about that specific pizza spatula was, after so many people had to use it to re-cut their slices, it had gained quite an edge. It was old, sure, but tools can only get old if they're built nice and sturdy. I picked it straight up and off the counter, avoiding the sound of sliding metal.

Obviously, pizza slicer versus gun isn't the best match-up, but I didn't intend to make it a fight. The key to sneaking up on someone is to understand the threshold of their attention. It isn't just eluding eye exposure, it's eluding anything that might alert them to the fact that things are about to go bad. A lot of people claim they have some kind of sixth sense, but it's really just tiny instances of common perception that go straight to their subconscious. If they never get those minuscule clues, they'll never suspect a thing.

The problem wasn't the lowlife with the pistol; he would have been easy if he was alone. The cashier, on the other hand, would have almost certainly shifted his eyes over to me when he saw me sneaking up, causing the gunman to turn around and turn me into Swiss cheese. I was crouched at the front of the aisle, a hair's width away from where he could have spotted me, when I launched my plan.

Due to the softness of the highly processed bread, and the tightness of the plastic, the shrink-wrapped egg sandwich didn't make a sound when I gingerly scooped it off of the shelf. Both my aim and my timing had to be perfect. I listened to the robber continue to threaten the cashier, then moved past his voice and focused in on the buttons on the cash register. There was a distinct rhythm to how he would press a button, realize it wasn't doing what he wanted it to, then try another one. I counted the beats, got myself in time, and chucked the sandwich across the store right as the cashier was looking down.

There wasn't much weight behind that sandwich, but there didn't need to be. It thudded against a bag of something on the other side of the store, and the gunman whipped himself around to face it. The cashier was looking in that direction as well, allowing me to make a silent yet brisk walk up to the robber's back.

He might have heard my footsteps as I got in close. He started to turn, but it was too late. The pizza spatula slid between the third and fourth of his cervical vertebrae. I twisted it, and his spine was in two separate pieces. He dropped like a rock, his blood pooling out onto the floor, his gun discharging into the window as it bounced on the ground.

"Sorry about the mess," I said to the cashier.

"Thank you," he stuttered out. "Please... Please wait here until the cops show up. You have to tell them what happened. What you did."

"That ain't very convenient." I smiled, stepping over the corpse and out the door.

PIZZA HELL

"I've got one place, but you ain't gonna like it."

"I don't have a choice, man. The bills don't pay themselves."

"Alright." A pause. "Little shop on 4th called 'Terrific's Pizza.' No reviews yet."

"No cheese alternatives either, I bet."

"Like I said, you ain't gonna like it."

"Thanks for the tip."

Frank hung up the phone and stored it in his right pocket. His notepad, with the words "Terrific's Pizza – 4th St." written on it, slid into his left. After several years of using his lactose-intolerant perspective to separate his reviews from the others, he had mostly run out of options. He didn't have the money to travel, and his informants were growing more reluctant with each conversation. They knew his relevance was fading, his gimmick growing tired. Given how important cheese is to most people's idea of pizza, he figured he would have to at least eat a bite of it to reach beyond his regular niche audience and make this review as profitable as possible. Until he could figure out a better solution, Frank decided it would be best to suffer a little sickness in exchange for potentially higher-paying reviews, and a restaurant that was yet untouched by his competition was like a gold mine.

Minutes later, Frank's car was slowly driving down 4th Street, searching for Terrific's Pizza. He didn't see any point in wasting time and, given that it was midday, he was feeling quite hungry. That hunger guided his eyes in their search for the establishment he hoped would solve his currently pressing problems. It didn't take long to find the place, but he nearly drove past it as a result of its indistinct appearance. Frank chuckled. The lack of reviews had been rationalized.

The building was small, square, and plain. The blinds were closed, and it wasn't entirely clear if the restaurant was open at all. The only indication that it even offered food was the tiny sign over the door, featuring a smiling cartoon chef and the words "TERRIFIC'S PIZZA." Parking his car a bit farther down the street, Frank got out and began mentally preparing himself. He knew that, depending on the size of the pizza, his view of the experience might be skewed by his inevitable dairy-induced affliction. Nevertheless, the circumstances called for operating outside of his usual perspective to a degree, even if that meant doing his best to ignore his own health.

He found the front door unlocked, and the interior tasteless. It was a child's image of a pizzeria, with red and white checkered cloths on the tables and various pizza-related paraphernalia tacked to the walls. Across the dining room, he could see the door to the kitchen, as well as two for the bathrooms, and one in-between, which he assumed was the office of the manager.

"Just one today?" called a voice, directing Frank to a short man standing off to his right. The man was dressed like a stereotypical waiter, complete with black vest and bow tie.

"Yeah, just me," Frank replied.

"Perfect. Take any seat you'd like."

The critic sat down at one of the tables in the middle of the room, hoping to better absorb the atmosphere of the pizzeria. His impression so far was better than many places he had been to in the past. The restaurant looked clean and the waiter seemed friendly, though there certainly wouldn't be any points awarded for creativity in their aesthetic. Frank was handed a menu.

Glancing through it, he was confused at

first, as it seemed to be nothing but a list of various toppings. He then noticed a small line at the top that read "Pizza - $10." The simplicity was refreshing but, combined with the generic surroundings, it made Frank think that the place was in serious need of personality. He decided it was time to figure some things out.

"Any specials?" he asked.

"Every pizza we make is special, sir," the waiter responded cheerfully.

"I see. What's the extra charge per topping?"

"None at all, as long as we can fit them all on."

"How are the pizzas cooked?"

"We use an oven that utilizes a combination of gas and wood. It's more efficient."

"Interesting."

"Thank you, sir. Are you, by chance, ready to order?"

He hadn't really thought about what kind of pizza he would like, as he was hoping they would have some kind of specialty, but he didn't need long to decide. He put in an order for a sausage and green pepper pizza, intending to evaluate their skill with both meat and vegetables while also keeping things simple. He asked for no cheese on all but one slice of the pizza, but the waiter said that would be "too precise for our methods." After some negotiation, he managed to get the waiter to agree to putting cheese on only half of the pizza. Thereafter, the waiter disappeared into the kitchen, and Frank was left alone. The waiter returned once to give him a glass of water, then withdrew again to the realm of cuisine.

A short while later, the waiter entered the room once more, carrying something that caused Frank to unintentionally let loose a burst of laughter. The pizza was significantly larger than any he had ever seen, and had a thickness to match. The waiter had a minor struggle bringing it to the table, and Frank had to hold his glass of water in order to clear enough room for it.

"Quite an impressive pizza for ten bucks," Frank remarked.

"Thank you, sir. We take pride in our work."

After setting the pizza down, the waiter walked over to the corner of the room and started cleaning tables. Frank set his drink on top of one of the other chairs at his table, and analyzed the monstrosity before him. It seemed to be a well-made pizza, with a crisp crust and properly cooked toppings. However, the sheer size was nightmarish. Frank was of fairly average height and weight, but he was confident that not even the hungriest and most spacious of men could conquer such a dish.

In addition, cheese was not only present on the entire pizza, but seemed to be layered well beyond ordinary pizza proportions. Frank smiled, thinking of how he could use that error to tear the restaurant down in his review. He didn't bother to ask the waiter about it, as he figured he was going to eat some portion of the pizza with cheese anyway, and the lack of accommodation would add some spice to his criticisms. Still, it was divided into slices, and Frank reasoned that one would be more than enough to write his review without getting too sick.

He pulled his chosen slice from the collective, and grimaced as the melted cheese formed strings between the two. He used his breath to cool down the pizza, then went in for his first bite. The flavor was phenomenal, overriding his psychological aversion to dairy for a brief moment and sending his mind to a dimension of pure bliss. It took him quite some time to finish that slice, both because of its size and his desire to savor each bite. There was a certain guilt when he took the last bit of crust into his mouth, already feeling full and sensing the nausea that would later overtake him. He called for the waiter.

"Yes, sir?" the waiter said, quickly moving to Frank's table.

"Could I get a box for this?" Frank asked. "I

think I'll have to finish it later."

The waiter, who had been nothing but jolly until this point, suddenly became unmistakably angry. His face contorted into a repulsed scowl, and he stared Frank down with intensity.

"We don't do that here," the waiter growled. "You'll have to finish it now."

"Are you kiddin' me? No one could finish a pizza like this!"

"Sir, are you insulting our establishment?"

Frank's attention was drawn by the opening of the kitchen door, through which two massive men in chef uniforms entered the dining area. They walked up to the side opposite the waiter at Frank's table, and he noticed that one of the chefs was carrying a large butcher knife.

"As I said," the waiter explained, "we take pride in our work. It would be very disrespectful, not to mention unwise, to leave that pizza uneaten in any measure."

"What is this?" Frank's voice grew louder. "You can't just threaten someone like that! I'm calling the police!"

He pulled his phone from his pocket, attempting to quickly dial the number of emergency services. Unfortunately for the restaurant critic, with only two digits dialed, the gargantuan chefs snatched the phone from his hands. The knifeless chef slammed it down on one of the nearby tables, and the other chef chopped it clean in half, burying his blade into the surface underneath. He ripped his knife out of the wood and looked over at Frank, giving him a wicked grin.

"Let's lock this punk down," the knifeless chef said.

"Excellent idea," the waiter replied, hurrying over to the door between the bathrooms and the kitchen.

When he opened that door, Frank tried to get a glimpse of what was inside. He could only see darkness, and was given little time to study it. The waiter stuck his head through the doorway for just a brief moment before exiting and closing the door once again. Then, the sound of metal scraping against metal echoed throughout the eatery, its oppressive volume causing Frank to cover his ears and hunker down.

The sound eventually stopped, and Frank straightened himself. The door through which he had entered, as well as all of the windows, now had thick walls of metal protecting them from floor to ceiling. He had become indefinitely trapped in a hackneyed pizzeria prison. Worse yet, his captors had no intention of simply leaving him with his thoughts.

"Pick up another slice," the chef with the knife said.

"Yeah," the other chef sneered. "Eat it before it gets cold. That would be bad, wouldn't it?"

Frank knew that taking another bite of the pizza would only intensify his impending illness, but defying the men might have resulted in something far worse. He had to think of a plan, and he had to do it fast. His lips trembled.

"I have to use the restroom," he stated as flatly as he could muster.

"No you don't," the waiter spat.

"Don't make us cut your tongue out, liar," the knife-wielding chef threatened.

"No, seriously!" Frank doubled down. "I have an intolerance to dairy products, and the cheese is getting to me! Do I have to spell it out?"

"He's bluffing," the other chef asserted.

"Big talk from the guy who probably won't have to clean it up," Frank said. Then, turning toward the waiter, "Let's hear what you have to say on it, sir."

"Alright, fine," the waiter replied. "But you better be back before that pizza goes bad, or you'll be living in there."

Deciding to ignore the odd threat from the

waiter, Frank hurried to the door labeled "MEN" and promptly locked himself into one of the three stalls therein. They were made of thin metal, and had massive gaps at the bottom. He understood that this position would only serve to trap him if they decided to attack now—he needed to think with haste.

Just the same, much to his dismay, nothing seemed to come to mind. He had no means of escape or communication, and the chefs would not be easily overpowered. Not only that, but Frank was fairly certain that they would not help him in the event that he actually did eat the whole pizza and suffer serious complications as a result. Frank was about to burst into tears when he heard a faint tapping on the wall of his stall.

His focus locked on it, then followed the noise downward as the taps went lower and lower. When they reached the gap in the stall, they abruptly stopped. Then, a gaunt and pale face slowly poked into his stall, peeking up at him from the floor. Stunned and unable to react, he watched bony fingers wrap around the dividing wall and pull an even bonier body toward him. Frank soon shared his stall with what appeared to be a naked, starving, ghoul of a man. Frank screamed.

"Pipe down, will ye?" The ghoul man snapped.

"What the hell is going on? What are you?" Frank stuttered.

"I'm what ye'll be if ye don't finish that pizza. Thought I could hide in here too, then my pizza went bad. Now the only thing I eat is scraps of onion from the kitchen at night."

Frank was practically hyperventilating at this point, overwhelmed by his situation.

"Calm down, wimp," the ghoul man continued. "We're gettin' out of here soon. I have a plan."

"Oh, fantastic. I don't think I could eat any more of that pizza."

"Well, that's a shame. I'm gonna need ye to eat more of that pizza. I'll sneak into the kitchen and keep the chefs busy, then ye can take the waiter one-on-one and hit the door switch in the manager's office."

"I don't know about all of this."

"Trust me, boy. Their guard is down. They already think they've got ye. Let's prove 'em wrong."

Frank exited the bathroom moments later, a strange confidence swirling within him. The waiter, having heard Frank's earlier scream, asked him if he met their "special guest" and the chefs broke into laughter. The restaurant critic did not respond. He did not meet their gaze. He took a deep breath, sat down, and began shoveling pizza into his mouth as fast as he could.

"That's more like it!" one of the chefs cheered.

"Must have scared him straight," added the other.

As the pizzeria employees watched Frank, the ghoul man slowly crept out of the bathroom and into the kitchen. The chefs' faces went from content to infuriated when they heard loud banging and rattling coming from their work space. As the ghoul man predicted, they left the waiter with Frank while they investigated the noise. The time had come.

"Keep eating," the waiter commanded. "Don't think you're getting o—"

Catching the waiter mid-sentence, Frank turned as he stood and landed a punch directly on the man's chin. It felt like he nearly broke his hand, but he couldn't afford to slow down. The waiter stumbled back in an attempt to recover. Frank picked up his chair and slammed it down over his jailer's head. The waiter was out cold, and Frank's path to the manager's office was clear.

Without hesitation, he approached the door between the bathrooms and the kitchen. It opened with ease, but still he saw only darkness inside. He knew the controls for the security system had to be in there somewhere, so he charged fearlessly into that abyss, losing all sight as the door shut behind him. He stumbled blindly for a while, then a dim light flickered on overhead.

"Frank Cane," a deep voice said gently. "We meet at last."

Frank scanned the freshly illuminated room. It seemed to be a typical little office, with a rug on the floor and a couple of chairs around a desk. Then Frank looked behind the desk, and saw a floating patch of shadow which resisted even the dispelling power of direct light. It shifted and morphed subtly, tendrils flicking out and retracting all around. It spoke again.

"It is a sad day when man must be made painfully aware of his weakness. His mortality."

Beyond fed up, Frank got directly to the point, saying, "I just want to leave. That's all."

"And leave you shall," the darkness replied. "But first, do tell of the lessons you learned today."

"I, uh, learned to never come back here again."

"Oh, Frank. How could you neglect to notice the rule of the strong and the subjugation of the weak? The complacency of man and his eventual downfall? The thickness of the crust?"

"Listen. I don't know what you are. I don't care about any of this. Please let me go home."

"This detention is nearly at its end, Frank.

You will find the front door open when you leave this room. But, my friend, there are conditions to your release."

"Go on."

"Your new companion has already become property of our domain. He shall be left with us. Furthermore, you are to write a review of this restaurant which will draw in a small amount of customers. Praise Terrific's Pizza, but not overly much. We need them to come one or two at a time, and you must use your expertise to achieve this."

Frank stood frozen for a while, nearly numb to shocking revelations. Nearly numb entirely. The shadowy manager knew his name. Not the one he published reviews under, but his real name. The one he hadn't told a soul in years. He reasoned it could likely find him and do something terrible to him if he didn't comply, and the police would be of little assistance. He would be living in anxious uncertainty for the rest of his life, but he didn't have much choice.

"All right," Frank said. "I'll do it."

"Smart choice. Now, be gone from this place. We have no more business at this time."

Walking out of the manager's office, Frank saw that the front door was indeed clear of obstruction as promised. He moved slowly, feeling the massive amount of pizza he had just eaten, mixed with the initial slice, starting to take its toll. He was sweating, and his body ached severely. He was almost to the door when he heard a shriek from the kitchen.

Frank desired nothing more than to escape, and could not imagine surviving long if the door were to again become inaccessible. But, part of him refused to leave. The ghoul man had saved him from potentially unending torment. It was his plan that allowed Frank to get this far. He felt bile in his throat, and struggled to hold it back. His feet changed directions.

When he pushed through the kitchen door, Frank discovered a scene of absolute chaos. The ghoul man had covered himself in oil, and was doing his best to wriggle his way out of the grasp of the chefs. They were punching him and slamming him against whatever they could, to little effect. Still, Frank could see in his new friend's eyes that the battle was already over. He was only fighting to waste more time.

"Hey, you overgrown mutants!" Frank yelled. One chef kept attacking the ghoul man while the other turned to face Frank.

"I finished your pizza," he continued, stepping closer. "Ready for my review?"

The chef opened his mouth to answer, and Frank lurched forward. Vomit spewed out of him at a high velocity, coating the chef's face and tongue, as well as a good deal of the other chef's body. They both shouted in disgust, and the chef holding the ghoul man loosened his grip slightly—just enough for him to get free.

In an instant, the ghoul man scooped up some of the vomit and rubbed it into both of the chefs' eyes. If Frank wasn't already spewing out the last of his stomach, he would have retched again at the grotesque sight. The chefs thrashed around blindly, unable to strike the slippery assailant upon them. As the ghoul man kept them distracted and sightless, Frank gradually recuperated from his expulsion session and became once more occupied with escape.

"Let's go!" he managed to say through panting breath.

"The gas line," the ghoul man shouted in reply. "Help me bust open the gas line on the oven!"

Too stressed for rational thought, Frank complied. The two of them pulled the oven away from the wall and the ghoul man ripped out the tube connecting it to the main gas line of the building. He then cranked the valve until the handle broke off, causing gas to be released into the room at a rapid pace. The chefs were still working on clearing their eyes when Frank and the ghoul man ran out of the kitchen and back into the dining area.

There, the waiter stood by the door, battered and enraged. He had awoken to see the door and windows uncovered and, not knowing the manager's intentions, came to believe that Frank had to be detained at all costs. From the sounds behind them, it was clear to the pair of potential escapees that the chefs had managed to regain their vision.

"We gotta shut the valve!" Frank heard one of the chefs yell.

"After we catch them. If they get out, it's all over!" the other chef replied.

They entered the dining area shortly after, trapping Frank and the ghoul man between themselves and the waiter. Seeing their opportunity preparing to pass them by, the ghoul man gave Frank a hard shove, causing him to stumble a few steps near the door. The waiter took advantage of this by punching Frank in the stomach, which made him double over and dry-heave. This was all according to the ghoul man's plan, as he vaulted over Frank's back and tackled the waiter. The two fell to the side, leaving the exit unprotected.

"Run!" the ghoul man shouted at Frank. "Get as far away as ye can!"

Frank wanted to argue. He wanted to believe he could save the man who saved him. But, in that moment of hesitation, he could hear the two chefs closing the distance from behind. He gave a solemn nod to his friend, then leapt through the door to freedom. He was weakened from his ordeal, but still ran to his car with all of the speed he could muster. He did not look back at Terrific's Pizza. He did not see the cartoon chef on the sign turn to watch him run away.

He reached his car, and felt a sting of panic when he could not find his keys. This passed quickly, as his hand soon found them deep in his pocket, and he started the car up without issue. Frank managed to drive about a city block away when it happened.

Terrific's Pizza exploded. Its walls blew open and its roof split skyward to accommodate the massive fireball expanding within it. Chunks of wood and metal blasted out and destroyed everything nearby. Frank felt his car shake, and did his best to keep driving straight. He silently mourned the man who freed him from that awful place, and through that he recognized that his job was not yet complete.

After arriving back home, Frank pulled his notebook from his left pocket. It was still open to the page where he had written "Terrific's Pizza - 4th

St." He took out a pen and drew a line underneath the name, indicating that he intended to give his thoughts. With trembling hands, Frank wrote his review:

"One out of five. Everything was burnt."

THE DESTINED DANCE OF OFFHAND OFFENDERS

The last recognizable thing I saw was the sea of people cheering us on. Then, lights and colors blended to a smear as strong hands ripped me off of the ground and into a painful German suplex. We had agreed to end the match with a suplex, but I sure as hell never told him to slam me that hard. Regardless, the audience loved it, and I thought it probably looked pretty good, so I couldn't get too mad about it. The Green Terror was a masked bastard in the ring, but he was my best friend and he knew how to work the crowd. If he wanted to beat me bloody, who was I to complain? Jack Magnum, best damn wrestler in the business, that's who. The rivalry between Green Terror and myself was the stuff of legends, and our eclectic mix of compromises and surprises in our bouts was the driving force behind it. Still, I wish I would have known that this would be the final match of my career.

After I got myself pinned by the suplex, we dealt with the typical post-show interviews and backstage reviews before returning to our respective hotel rooms. We were only supposed to stay in Chicago for another night before traveling to Salt Lake City, but there were some complications in the scheduling, so we were gonna be stuck until things straightened out. I didn't blame the promoters—still don't to this day. I'm surprised we even had work at all, considering the circumstances.

Two days before my match with the Green Terror, the whole world flipped its lid. Around Turquoise Lake in Colorado, middle of the day, this big earthquake broke out. The bottom of the lake opened up with a bang so loud that eardrums were bursting twenty miles away, forcing the eyes to watch in silence as the water drained down the fresh abyss. Like I said before, I was in Chicago at the time, but I swear I heard it. I felt it. And I watched, live on television, as some colossal beast of bone and steel came rising out of that hole in Turquoise Lake.

The newscasters were speechless, and the ominous aura of their hush bled through into my hotel room, making it so cold that I began to shake. This thing was at least a hundred feet tall, and it was shaped like an uncannily perfect human. It had the proportions of the goddamn Vitruvian man, but with the bulging physique of an Olympic weightlifter. Its skin was a mesh of metallic cables, weaving through and around thick ribs which intersected and protruded all across its body. Its face was a single stoic slab, lips together and calm. This mysterious monster climbed up out of the lake, looked around, and started walking dubiously slow toward the southwest. People were losing their minds, the government exploded in confusion, and every other nation had its eyes glued to the United States with fearful anticipation.

I was doing fine. As it turns out, there ain't much like a couple of dudes pummeling the shit out of each other when it comes to taking someone's mind off of something, and ten bucks for a light beer sounds better and better as the night goes on. My big match in Chicago made me feel like I was actually contributing something to society for once, rather than working to get paid. My parents always thought that I would be a doctor or a lawyer, but I figured, if I really had a good brain on me, I could find a way to make a difference while getting my head smashed onto a turnbuckle.

Anyway, being that the trip to Salt Lake City was temporarily suspended, I cooled down from my hard day of work by flipping through local programs and eating vending machine food in my hotel room. At around one in the morning, while I was watching some guy's homemade music video, my door received a couple of firm knocks. I opened it up, and a rookie wrestler immediately walked on in without even saying anything. He was a nice enough guy, but you just don't do that. It goes against common courtesy, my own privacy, and the manners expected of a beginner around veterans.

"What the fuck?" I couldn't help but yell.

"Sorry, dude, shit is going down right now. Rob said he would meet me here in a bit."

I paused for a moment to consider this interaction. This punk had no problem calling Green Terror by his real name, but I was relegated to "dude"? I guess it might have been because I never used his name when I addressed him, but his name was Wolfhammer, and that's fucking stupid— at least to me. He thought it was so cool that he changed his full legal name to it. One name. One word. Ridiculous.

"Why d'you got your TV on but it ain't on the news? Wake up!"

I prepared to teach Mr. Wolfhammer's face a lesson, reaching down to pick up the handset from the hotel telephone. Fortunately for my criminal record, Rob walked in right at that moment, and

the desire diffused. We were both in our mid-
thirties, but he was looking twice as old that night.
He had been watching the news since he got to the
hotel, and the stress it caused him was pulling his
posture into a feeble slouch. The three of us were
the only wrestlers staying in that particular hotel, so
I suppose it was natural for him to bring us together
in one room. I don't get why it had to be my room
without telling me, but that's another drop in the sea
of bullshit at this point.

An awkward atmosphere presented itself as
we all found seating on the edge of my queen-size
bed. Television now firmly locked on national news,
we saw the familiar titan in a shroud of darkness,
revealed by its outline against the ambient lights
of the sky. The broadcast was being filmed from a
helicopter high above, giving us a bird's-eye view
of the thing as it continued to meander around
the Rocky Mountains. However, it stopped when
it reached Mount Massive, and I could no longer
hear Rob and Wolfhammer breathing. The creature
buried its fingertips into the mountainside and
proceeded to tear off a large chunk of rock like it
was putty.

"It's been doing this all day, apparently,"
Rob said in a low voice. "Government's talking
about blasting it with missiles, bunch of peaceful

protesters are causing trouble, and now there's a big political battle going on between all these people trying to figure out what to do with it. I've even heard a couple of experts say that other countries might attack us while we're all disorganized."

"No way that would happen, right?" Wolfhammer asked me, begging for his mind to be eased by my elderly wisdom.

"Have you talked to the other guys on this tour?" I asked Rob, leaving Wolfhammer to his mental torment as punishment for earlier events.

"I talked to Brad, who tried to relay my message to the other guys, but half of them won't take phone calls or visitors, and that new guy we signed last week is out sleeping in his car somewhere."

"What did Brad say?" I inquired with genuine curiosity. Brad Bigman was the longest running name in the game, and we all looked up to him like a five-hundred-pound father.

"He said 'there ain't shit we can do but wait' then cracked open a beer and chugged it with the phone still next to his mouth."

"Classic Brad."

At that moment, the reporter in the helicopter told us that she would have them fly in for a closer look, so our attention shifted back to the screen. There was a dense tension as the helicopter turned on its searchlight, but the beast didn't seem to notice, so we were treated to an in-depth look at its nighttime activities. It was in a seated position, with the stone from the mountain on its lap. It had sliced one side so that it was completely flat, and was using its index finger to carve basic shapes into the fresh visage. The creature began with a large rectangle, in which it attempted to engrave what looked like words, but its finger was too thick for the required precision and the end result was a muddled mess. It then made a line of shorter, wider rectangles going out from the original one horizontally on both sides. Finally, it traced the outline of the whole community of shapes, freeing them from the surrounding rock and creating a bulge in the middle to act as a centerpiece. The realization hit me like a lariat.

"Fuck!" I shouted without thinking. "Do you see that, boys?"

"Yeah. Like I said, it's been doing this all day," Rob replied.

Neither of them understood. I had no idea how they didn't, but they didn't. I suddenly felt like it was a secret message meant for me alone. Like that big behemoth was speaking right into my mind, and it wanted a reply.

"I'm going to Colorado," I stated as I stood to pack my things.

"Excuse me?" Wolfhammer said in disbelief. "Do you see how dangerous that thing is? Do you think you'll walk up to it, give it one of your signature chokeslams, and save the day?"

"You'll die like an idiot and I won't go to your funeral," Rob added with the slightest hint of sarcasm.

"That thing ain't dangerous—I think. It doesn't want to kill me, and it doesn't want me to kill it."

I took a deep breath as I closed the last zipper on my travel bag.

"It wants a championship."

Ten minutes later, I was in the lobby of the hotel, trying to figure out how to get to the nearest overnight car rental. Naturally, Wolfhammer followed and Rob appeared shortly after. The bratty novice was loudly chewing me out, pretending to be giving advice as a friend while actually overstepping his bounds and making my hands squeeze into very tight fists.

Strangely, Rob didn't say anything in all of this. He watched and waited as Wolfhammer threw his little tantrum and woke up half of the hotel guests. Then, Rob stepped forward and placed his left leg behind Wolfhammer's right knee, hooked his arm around the punk's neck, and pulled him backward, throwing him to the ground while continuing to walk in a single fluid motion. That was when I saw that Mr. Green Terror had a travel bag of his own on his shoulder.

"Learn some respect," he said with disdain. Rob was always more of a man of action than words when he was pissed off. Maybe that's why we understood each other so well.

We thus left the hotel and set on our journey to the airport. I told Rob about my plan to get a rental car and felt more than a little stupid when he informed me how much faster it would be to wait a couple of hours for a flight. We could not go back to the hotel. Even though Wolfhammer was a rookie, he was still associated with the wrestling company, and we had decisively disgraced that company in our leaving. We knew damn well that we would be fired on the spot once they found out that we disobeyed the order to stay in Chicago, but we had enough confidence in our skills to think that a different promotion would pick us up later on. Of course, we were really nothing more than a couple of cocky morons, retiring in our prime.

Eight hours later, having flown to Colorado Springs and then taken a rental car the rest of the way, we arrived at the entrance to a trail leading to Mount Massive. Between the two of us we had only managed about five hours of sleep, but we were accustomed to going a few days with limited rest. The small parking lot for the nature trail was packed with cars, and people could be seen in all directions trying to somehow catch a glimpse of the monster seven miles away. Armed soldiers had been stationed all around the mountain's access points to ensure that none of these people accidentally did something that the government hadn't finished arguing about yet. We parked a bit farther up the road and prepared a plan.

"Well, we tried," Rob said with a sigh.

"Oh, come on," I replied. "We're big-time famous right now. All we gotta do is find a soldier that looks like they're into wrestling."

"There is no way someone is gonna let us into that guarded area just because we hurt each other on television."

"Shut up, nerd. Help me look."

We studied the faces of the nearby soldiers, staying in the car to reduce suspicion. We discovered that there wasn't much to gain from doing this, so we got out and went walking along the line of attentive camouflage—trying to act as if we had a destination in mind somewhere down the road. Finally, I saw what I needed. A greasy teenager with a rifle that was far too big for him did a double take as he noticed us approaching. I adjusted my path and made a beeline for the kid. Rob followed suit.

"Hey, buddy," I said to him nonchalantly, making him jump in surprise.

"Jack Magnum," he stammered. "Are you Jack Magnum?"

"That's right. You ever meet a champion in person before?"

"But, um, I mean, Jack Magnum's never won a title before, I'm pretty sure. He was supposed to win one but the Green Terror stole it I think. I don't know. I'm a huge fan but I'm not sure."

"Not me, you jokester," I laughed while grabbing Rob's arm and beginning to gradually circle around the starstruck youth. "This guy right here is the champion. You ever see the Green Terror without his mask on?"

The kid's jaw dropped. No one knew what the Green Terror actually looked like at that point, and it would have been quite the shock to see him hanging out with his lifelong nemesis. That's why Rob wore the mask in the first place, really. We became friends back when we both wrestled for small independent groups, and he performed maskless as "Rob Ripper." When he ended up signed to the same professional organization as me later on, he somehow convinced the creative department to turn him into a masked heel out to ruin my life. I didn't even know it was him until our third match.

"Anyway," I continued, now fully behind the line of guards and beginning to back up into the forest, "whoever's in charge of all this, I don't know their name, they talked to our agents and arranged for us to meet them near where that big monster is hanging out for some reason. They were supposed to tell you guys but I guess they might not have yet."

"Oh, that's weird. I didn't hear anything about that. Let me radio this in and confirm it real quick."

"Listen man, we're in a hurry here. We were supposed to be there an hour ago but one of your buddies down the road was fucking with us, calling wrestling 'lame' and searching our pockets even though we're here on orders that go above him. Total asshole."

"Really?"

"Yeah, man. I'm glad we met you, I was starting to think that all military guys are stiff pricks. Let us on through and I promise you'll be commended later. Trust me. Jack Magnum, the master of the squared circle, never lies and never, ever, breaks a promise."

By this time, Rob and I were already well enough away from him. I gradually moved faster and faster backward before ultimately turning around and walking on as normal into the wood. The young soldier never said anything back to me, but he didn't stop us either. Making that guy go through such a mental conflict honestly had me feeling down for a minute. I then remembered the great feat I had accomplished as a result of that conflict, and my despair was drowned in an ocean of pride. An hour after these internal happenings, Rob spoke up.

"Alright, bud, you gotta level with me. How did that terrible plan actually work?"

"No plan is terrible with Jack Magnum at the helm," I replied. "Even if he's playin' it by ear."

"Do you think we'll run into more military personnel around here?"

"There might be some on patrol somewhere, but I'm betting they're not allowed to go as close to the beast as we already are. This whole situation is a real gray area. As far as I'm concerned, there's no problem with simply walking forward until something stops us. We're two dumb tourists who somehow got lost in the woods despite there being guards around the perimeter, you get it?"

"Jack, I'm gonna pray that we don't get shot so that I can kick your ass later."

We continued on without words, listening to the solid thuds of our feet against the hard dirt, garnished with the occasional snap of a twig. I've had countless people tell me how great the air is in the wilderness, all crisp and aromatic and so on. That day, I found out that they were all liars. The air was thick, hard to breathe, and it smelled like a reckless pyrotechnics show. There was also a heavy heat that seemed to come in waves, pulsating out from some place up ahead. I had a feeling that these were signs of our proximity to the behemoth, but I knew for sure when we began to hear the alien sounds of its movement. They were short bursts which came in rapid succession—not like footsteps, more like popping knuckles.

Undeterred by these omens, we reached the point where the forest ended. Having nothing to block our line of sight in the mountainous terrain, the creature came into view. It was standing in a relatively flat clearing, holding a championship belt it had crafted from stone in one hand while it employed the other to do various victory poses. The ribs which protruded from its body clacked together and pulled apart during these motions, creating the odd sound we had previously been treated to. I thought it was pretty intimidating on the news, but in real life it was on a whole new level. I could feel a primal fear surging within me, and a rush of excitement came with it. The sound of blood in my veins became the only thing that I could hear, and a voice in my mind was telling me to flee without using language. It reminded me of the first time I wrestled in a real ring. I couldn't stop smiling.

There was a helicopter far off in the distance, probably getting more footage for reporters to gawk at. It looked like they were too far away to see us, though I wouldn't have cared much if they could. Rob stayed back by the trees as I advanced toward the massive entity with a steady pace, observing the subtle vibrations of its sinuous mesh skin. When I was about a hundred and fifty feet away from the thing, it noticed me. It stopped posing and stood with a neutral stance, tilting its head slightly downward to look at me directly. Its stone belt fell to the ground, breaking into several pieces with an echoing crash. Any semblance of a strategy I once had was, at this point, gone. I acted on instinct.

"What's up, big guy?" I yelled. It didn't react, so I kept talking. "You like wrestling, don't you? I'm kind of a wrestler myself. I wish we were in the same weight class so I could test you out. Hey! Hello? Can you even hear at all?"

Having calmed down to the point of being able to think again, I silently berated myself for acting like a jackass. I could feel Rob's eyes on my back, and I knew he was calling me a goddamn idiot in a voice too low for me to hear. Nonetheless, I felt like something in the way it was standing was telling me that it was on the same page as me to a certain degree. Maybe it didn't fully grasp my words, but I got the sense that it knew who I was.

"Rob!" I called out, refusing to take my eyes off of the beast. "Come over here."

"Absolutely not."

"Come on man, this is the crucial moment. This thing has a craving for wrestling, I know it. We gotta show it the best that wrestling has to offer. Faces and heels, man. We gotta show it Jack Magnum and the Green Terror."

Whether compelled by my words or determined to be killed instead of listening to them, Rob walked out to meet me. He was hesitant to get as close to the giant as I was, but he came around after a few minutes. It was time to put on a private show for our potential new fan.

"Alright Rob, activate the Green Terror."

"I don't have my mask, I left it in the car."

"What the hell are you talking about? Just do the moves."

"I can't get in the right mindset without something covering my face."

"Jesus Christ, man. Pull your shirt over your face."

"What? Why? Also, shouldn't you have your shirt off? That's how you wrestle."

"I'm taking my fucking shirt off so pull yours over your goddamn face HOLY FUCK!"

We went on like this for a few more minutes, until we reached the desired state of myself being shirtless and Rob having his own shirt covering his face. He couldn't see much of anything, so we decided to showcase one quick finisher and get it over with. Rob charged at me, I dodged at the last moment, then he turned around and charged again. When he reached the proper distance, I fully extended my arm to put a hand around his neck and he jumped up and a little backward to stop his momentum. Then, we worked together to turn him onto his back in midair before I brought down my arm and slammed him into the harsh ground. A beautiful chokeslam.

The monster, though it could not emote, made its opinion on our display obvious. It began to fidget in place, as if it did not know what to do with itself, then got down on one knee and bowed its head. A sign of reverence. Once again, my brilliant planning abilities and spontaneous wit had saved the day.

The next few hours were spent figuring out how to communicate with our new friend. We found that it was very good with gestures, and through those I managed to teach it a few words like "wrestle" and "belt." It wasn't capable of speaking, but it could point at the remnants of its stone championship belt and get into a wrestling stance when I said the appropriate word. We didn't have a lot going for us, but we were making it work. As time went on, the creature's soul fraternized more and more with my own, and the two had much in common. I wouldn't even know where to begin with explaining how a living scrapyard from below the Earth's surface developed a desire for a championship title, but it happened, and there was no mistaking it. At that time, I figured if it was gonna be a long while before I ever even got a shot at a title again, I might as well give this thing a shot at its own. One of us had to get what we wanted.

"Hey, pal," I said to the beast as it stared wistfully at its crumbled belt. "You want the real thing? Tell you what, I'll be your promoter, and your coach, and I'll make sure you take home the biggest, most extravagant belt ever made."

It probably didn't get most of what I said, but it liked how I talked about the belt with a positive tone, and it knew that the ones it was making out of mountains were merely imitations, so we were pretty much good to go. That said, before I did anything with the world's largest wrestler, I needed to give it a ring name.

"Rob, what should we call this thing?"

"Mega Trashcan, or something. I don't know," he replied without even looking over at me, apparently fatigued from helping teach my intensive and impromptu English course.

"Fuck off, man, be serious. We gotta call it something that's, like, badass, but not scary, because it's scary enough already. People don't like being scared too hard."

"Well, people like mythology, and for all we know this thing could be straight out of some ancient legend, so give it a name related to that."

Rob's contribution, while minimal, managed to spark my creativity. Images of gods and heroes that I had read about in high school swirled around in my head as I tried to narrow down the list to a solitary name. I failed to match anything up based on appearance, but there was one name that kept coming back to me. A name fitting for something that would change humanity forever. I pointed at the colossal creature and delivered my message slowly, ensuring that it grasped the meaning.

"You. Are. Prometheus."

With that, I officially picked up the first and last client of my management career. Over the following week, Rob and I slept in the woods and taught Prometheus as much as we could about wrestling, entertainment, and the English language. It figured out new moves almost instantly, and had a great work ethic. Of course, this had not gone unnoticed by the government, the news, or our old wrestling family. Multiple "negotiators" and "peacekeepers" approached us one at a time, bringing food and water to pacify us in an attempt to get a hint at what was going on. They always left confused after we devoured their offerings and told them that we were practicing wrestling. At some point, our former promotion, along with the other wrestlers under their command, started working with the government to give them a better idea of who we were and what we might be plotting. Shortly after that, a refreshing countenance came to visit our training camp. It was perched atop an impressively oversized body, and held a slight smile which curled into a smirk as it drew closer.

"What have you numbnuts gotten yourselves

into?" Brad Bigman said, sipping a beer from the six-pack he had brought with him.

We tried to explain the ambitions of our sizable student, but he clearly wanted only to rant at us about how the government was pissed off and wouldn't leave him alone. Luckily, genius struck yet again. I proposed to Brad that Rob and I also join forces with the government, utilizing their resources to give Prometheus what it would think to be actual wrestling matches, allowing it to achieve its dream of becoming a champion. Surprisingly, Brad was into it. He pulled a little radio transceiver out of his pocket and, ten minutes later, we were face to face with a group of powerful politicals in the nearby woods. I told them that Prometheus wouldn't attack them, but they remained unwilling to leave the protective shroud of trees.

Once it was firmly established that we weren't terrorists and that our wrestler was totally tame, the whole party got along nicely. Since the government still hadn't worked out a long-term plan for the situation, they agreed to aid in appeasing Prometheus for the time being so as to avoid further unsanctioned mountain carving. We arranged for a tour of bouts heading east, ending—if we had built enough trust by then—in New York City. Our wrestler was too tall for the illustrious

Madison Square Garden, but we got Central Park as a consolation. They also promised a championship belt that would actually fit our behemoth, complete with giant gemstones and the word "CHAMPION" printed in gold. In exchange, I was to be in charge of keeping Prometheus out of trouble, while Rob was to handle giving status updates to the suits and keeping me out of trouble. It sounded like a great deal and, at the time, we were flying high.

The first match of Prometheus' career took place on a square patch of concrete outside of Denver, where the government had stacked three metal shipping containers up to be the same height as the beast. With the containers in the center of the square, and Prometheus on an outer edge, everything was ready to go. A huge crowd had gathered around the perimeter of the concrete, again held back by camouflaged gunslingers, but eager to see my student in action. Promoters can't really ask for much more than a client that comes with their own fans. I grinned as I thought about adding "Highly Successful Athlete Management" to my résumé. Moments later, this grin receded as Rob handed me a megaphone. The time had come.

"Ladies and gentlemen!" I yelled, unconsciously entering my wrestling persona. "I am Jack Magnum—Yes, THE Jack Magnum—and

I'm here to show you the FUTURE of professional wrestling!"

Following its cue, Prometheus flexed its massive arms, and the crowd roared. I held my tongue until the cheering subsided.

"For the first time ever, the FIRST and ONLY wrestler in the all-new GARGANTUAN HEAVYWEIGHT CLASS will display its devastating techniques and indomitable spirit. Weighing in at way too damn heavy, from Parts Unknown... PROMETHEUS!"

Again according to plan, Prometheus stepped into the concrete ring and hunkered down into a wrestler's stance. The match was about to begin when I heard the whine of another megaphone turning on.

"And representing our beautiful country the United States of America, weighing in at twelve and a half tons, THE ALAMO!"

Wolfhammer emerged from behind the shipping containers to a deluge of applause. That son of a bitch. I knew right away that I had been deceived, and that there was no way we were getting a shot at that belt once Prometheus became the villain. This match had suddenly revealed itself as the one to decide it all. If we couldn't win the crowd here, there would be nothing to look forward to other than federal prison for conspiring with an unpatriotic entity. I motioned for Prometheus to lean down to me, and I gave it all the advice I had.

"Don't fucking listen to 'em," I said with fire. "The only thing that matters is kicking ass, hard and fast. Let me tell you what Brad told me the first time I had a serious show in front of a serious audience: focus on one thing. Keep yer eyes right on that Alamo fucker and nothing else will matter, nothing else will exist. You know these people want to see some action. Always give the crowd what they want, and then a bit more for good measure. Once the bell rings, don't stop until you got nothing left."

There wasn't really a reaction to what I said, but it made me feel better to say it. One of the suits on the sidelines produced a ring bell, and my wrestler got back into its proper posture. The spectators doubled their volume as the bell rang and the first Gargantuan Heavyweight bout commenced.

Prometheus charged forward, diving through the middle container and knocking the top one to the side. Met with a mixture of boos and cheers, it turned around and continued battering the containers with dropkicks, powerbombs, and body presses, until whoever was acting as referee hit the bell and called the match—win by TKO.

Prometheus lifted its arms in victory, but the cheers had entirely turned to jeers, angry at the way the American wrestler had been treated. Things were looking bad, but my wrestler was quick to adapt, bending down and picking up parts of The Alamo without turning toward the crowd. It must have gotten my earlier message.

From there, us humans once again watched as the titan got down to business. It crushed, shaped, and twisted the shipping containers at a leisurely rate, creating awful metal screeches that easily defeated the audience's auditory assault. We were witnessing improvisational genius. When the screeches stopped, three sharp bangs signaled that Prometheus had set all of the containers in their final places. The cheering began again—slowly but surely, unhindered by booing, building to a deafening ovation. Prometheus had mangled the shipping containers into the letters "U," "S," and "A."

Somehow, this turned out to be one of the most renowned moments in wrestling history. It was as if we had revealed that my wrestler was the real United States wrestler, and The Alamo was a mockery made by some crafty thugs. The government was flipped into the antagonist of its own story. Rob and I had a lot of fun listening to them panic on their little radios, having a frantic back-and-forth with our former promoter, who could offer only a nervous reassurance.

Despite their concerns, we had put on a good show, so we packed our things and moved to the next one—set to be in St. Louis. Rob and I were transported on taxpayer dime with planes, cars, and even helicopters. Usually we would ride with Brad, but Wolfhammer sometimes invited himself along as well, making us all feel tense and tight-lipped. Prometheus simply ran on foot, escorted by government planes and following the path cleared by ground agents. The thing was unbelievably quick, too—almost always arriving at around the same time as us.

The St. Louis show went about as well as the first one, but it didn't sit right with me. Our opponent was another pile of shipping containers, this time named "Boston Tea Party" or "BTP." From there, we would face "Lexington" in Indianapolis and "Concord" in Philadelphia—again, shipping containers. Each show would draw more fans than the last, but I could tell that they expected something more. Who the hell ever heard of a wrestler that just broke things? Even though we were cleared for our final match in New York City, it didn't feel like a championship at all. As we drove out to Central Park, I began seething in my seat, realizing too late the predicament we had gotten ourselves into. The government was afraid of Prometheus' success, so they were sandbagging it to save face. In other words, they had no respect for us or the art of wrestling.

We arrived at the heart of Central Park, driving through the grass without worry of reprimand. Prometheus was nearby, having slowly navigated the city with its entourage of blacked-out Cadillacs. Meanwhile, Rob and I were stuck with yet another rental car, though we at least weren't paying for it. With the massive crowd staring us down like ravenous wolves, my anger reached its peak. I saw the stack of metal they were about to call our number one contender, probably giving it some stupid name like "Pearl Harbor." I refused to let it end like this. I rolled down my window, grabbed Rob's megaphone, and used it to tell Prometheus to pick us up and take us out of there. Rob pretended to be all worked up about it, but I could tell that he was mad about the same thing I was.

I instructed Prometheus to take us into the East River, then head south. As we passed the crowd, I exclaimed "Get your asses to Upper Bay! Liberty State Park! Fucking Governors Island!"

and they scrambled to comply. Trudging through the water, my wrestler carried us out to Ellis Island, where it set us down according to my word. None of the people who had been at the park were there yet, but plenty of others had already formed a new crowd on every piece of land in sight.

Shouts of confusion rang out from Rob's transceiver, and hundreds of government and military vehicles began to swarm from all angles. It was too late to stop us. There were too many innocent people around, and the country was in love with our antics. They had no choice but to sit back and watch me make my own championship fight. At that point, I was tired, I was homeless, and I definitely could have been called tempest-tost. Without even knowing if the people watching would be able to hear me, I raised the megaphone and spoke.

"I've decided to take matters into my own hands. Watch closely, you disrespectful cretins! The Gargantuan Heavyweight Championship will conclude right here, right now, with a match between Prometheus and Lady Liberty herself. We're going to destroy the false idols of old and show you who the REAL Americans are!"

The next few minutes were like a dream. Prometheus, at my command, rushed across

Upper Bay and onto Liberty Island, where it then climbed the pedestal on which the Lady stood. It wrapped its arms around her upper body and pulled, breaking the statue at the ankles with a groaning snap and flipping the detached portion up over its head as it jumped backward off of the platform. An exquisite superplex. Lady Liberty's entire body slammed into the brick walkway, while Prometheus landed carefully on its backside. Her copper shell was cracked and ruined, and she had been split into several large chunks. Recovering from the superplex, Prometheus got its legs around the chunk which still had Lady Liberty's head and outstretched arm attached to it, breaking the arm off as it was pulled into an armbar. The whole world seemed to go dead. I wasn't sure if my stunt had actually done anything or not. Then, Rob ran up to me with his transceiver, claiming that I needed to talk to someone on it. It was a voice I didn't recognize, so I knew it was some dickhead in a suit.

"Jack, that wasn't very smart."

"What the hell are you gonna do about it?" I barked in response.

"Tell ya what, you want a real fight? You want a real championship? I'll give you one. Meet me in Central Park in one week. Don't leave the city, and keep that monster right the fuck where it is. Deal?"

"Deal. But when I win, you guys gotta leave all of us alone. Make us go to Canada or something, but don't ever fuck with us, or any of the other wrestlers, ever again. Deal?"

There was a long pause. Then, "Deal."

I didn't do much for the next three days. I was jazzed-up over the victory and, honestly, I forgot all about the conversation with the anonymous dickhead. Prometheus stood on the pedestal that once held Lady Liberty, and I spent a lot of time hanging out with it, telling my best wrestling stories while confused citizens watched from afar. Outside of that, Rob and I were staying in some fancy hotel, ordering room service and messing around in the pool. However, it was on that third day that a little punk with a stupid name had to show up and spoil the fun.

"Are you guys taking this seriously?" Wolfhammer yelled. "Those feds aren't fucking around anymore!"

"Why should we tell you?" Rob asked, stabbing his spoon into a masterfully crafted chocolate sundae.

"Uh, because we're on the same side, bro. We're family."

"Bull-fucking-shit," I interrupted. "You've

been on their side the whole time."

"I thought we were working an angle," he said without a hint of deception. "I thought everyone was in on it."

"You mean to tell me that you accidentally got yourself on the enemy team, with access to insider info, because you thought it was part of a planned storyline?" I sneered.

"Yeah."

"How can we trust you?" Rob asked bluntly.

"Considering the situation I've now come to understand, I don't think you can. But, if you guys can head over to our New York recording studio, there are some guys ready to work who already know the drill. I know it's short notice, but if you can manage to cut a promo by the end of tomorrow, I guarantee you that I can give you what you need to win this fight."

He left right after saying that, but his presence hung in the air. We talked for a while about Wolfhammer's allegiances, then resolved to do as he suggested. When we arrived, we indeed did find some engineers and producers that had worked with me on promos in the past. Within minutes, I was set up between a camera and the fake alleyway we often used as a background, microphone in hand. As I was about to call for filming to begin, Rob walked into frame. He was shirtless, and had the word "RIPPER" written on his chest in red paint. I smiled and signaled to the cameraman. The golden age had returned.

"People of the United States of America," I said coldly, "it has come to my attention that some shady gang of extremists out there is trying to bring Prometheus down."

"NOT gonna happen," Rob interjected.

"To make sure of it, I've brought back an old ghost from my past. So, you KNOW there won't be any funny business, because Jack Magnum and Rob Ripper are going to STOMP those ambitions into the dirt, and Prometheus WILL take home the Gargantuan Heavyweight Championship belt."

"Yer gettin' a clean fight, and whatever sorry stack of shipping containers you put in the ring is gonna wish it never messed with a REAL wrestler."

"Say your prayers while you can." I dragged my finger across my throat, then pointed it straight down. "Central Park is where you'll be buried."

We ended the video there, and the studio guys went straight into editing it for television. They knew we didn't have much time left, and I'm guessing that they were paid a large amount by our old promotion to help us out. In that way, I suppose we kind of were like a family—Rob and I being the black sheep. We were all jerks to each other at one time or another, but the company always helped us out when we needed it, and we always put on a good show in return. Perhaps this was their way of reminding us that we still had obligations. We still had one more performance.

Due to the tireless efforts of the studio crew, the promo aired the next day. I heard good things about it, but nothing drastic seemed to happen as a result. On the day before the true championship bout, I had become certain that Wolfhammer tricked us. I was watching television in my hotel room, plotting to beat the shit out of him the next day in a way that would look staged, when my own face appeared on the screen. I used to like watching my old promos, so I turned up the volume and relaxed.

"People of the United States of America, it has co—"

The screen cut to black, then a new image appeared. Wolfhammer and Brad Bigman were standing in front of a huge humanoid robot—something out of science fiction. It looked to be about the same height as Prometheus, and its skin was made of plates of metal which overlapped like armor.

"That's enough of that crap," Brad said.

"Yeah," Wolfhammer added. "No one wants

to hear trash talk from a bunch of trash."

"See this model of perfection behind me? It's called The Constitution, and it's the last thing your puny Prometheus is ever going to see. It moves fast, hits hard, and, if that ain't enough, it has rocket propulsion systems in its arms and legs."

"Don't forget missiles that shoot from its chest! The Constitution has 'em, and Prometheus doesn't. This fight isn't even fair."

"Jack, Rob, we used to be pals. Maybe we can put this all behind us after the fight, if you can call me from Hell."

The video cut there, as Brad reached down out of frame and the opening of a pressurized can could be heard. Those lunatics had actually done it. They had convinced the government to let them cut a promo in response to ours, and managed to reveal our opponent's secrets in the process. I don't know how many times that commercial aired before it was pulled down, but the damage was already done. Prometheus was still stationed out at Liberty Island, but I would be able to get it up to speed before the match. I was electrified with excitement. I wanted that belt.

The day of the final match arrived, and all of the key players gathered in Central Park. Four great poles had been placed in a square formation, with thick cords stretched around them to create a wrestling ring for giants. The Constitution was waiting in the ring, inactive but ready for orders. It had a glorious title belt, fit to my specifications, secured tightly on its waist with bolts—as if it were already champion. I told Prometheus what it needed to know, then left it to do its own thing. I was confident in my student. Once both fighters were in the ring, some greasy teenager in a helicopter above did the introductions, his squeaking yet dedicated voice booming through speakers all around the park. The Constitution seemed to wake up at the sound of its name, getting into a wrestler's pose to match Prometheus. The sound of a bell soon followed, and the rest was in the hands of fate.

Standing at opposite corners, The Constitution wasted no time in firing a barrage of missiles at Prometheus as soon as the match was officially underway. My wrestler dodged what it could, but ended up taking a few missiles to the arms and chest, breaking off some spines and melting holes into the system of metal cables. Prometheus then ran in for a dropkick, but the rocket-propelled arms of The Constitution caught its legs and flipped it onto its head, scoring several rocket-propelled kicks on Prometheus' body as it struggled to a standing position.

"Use the ropes!" I yelled, hoping to be of some help.

Prometheus seemed to hear me, as it ran again at The Constitution, this time ducking under a stiff-armed swing and continuing straight past the dangerous droid. It then caught itself on the ropes and flipped its momentum back the other way, crashing into The Constitution before it had time to turn around. Prometheus attempted to go for a pinning hold, but its opponent utilized the rockets in its legs to kick out. The Constitution was the first one back to its feet, and it took advantage of this by creating some distance between the two and firing another missile volley at my unprotected student.

This time, there was no dodging or even blocking. The missiles blasted Prometheus directly, destroying sections of exterior all over its body and sending it stumbling backward into the ropes. It was impossible to see or hear it, but my wrestler was crying in pain, and I knew there was severe internal damage. This couldn't go on for much longer.

"End this in one move!" I shouted. "You have to go for a finisher!"

The opposing wrestler, possibly out of missiles, moved in to fight up close. Prometheus was slumped and motionless. Precisely when The Constitution was about to go for a grab,

Prometheus ducked and hopped out of the way. I couldn't believe it had mastered the art of feigning exhaustion so fast. The Constitution, now holding the ropes, turned once more to face its enemy. Before it could get to grappling with its arms again, Prometheus stepped forward, put a hand around its neck, and lifted. The Constitution was now being held in the air by its neck, unable to break free despite assailing the lifting arm with rocket-propelled punches. As it is significantly more difficult to complete a chokeslam when the other party doesn't consent to it, Prometheus had to shift its body in preparation. At that moment, The Constitution activated all of the rockets in its legs.

The two were slowly raised into the air, both refusing to relent. There was a grand struggle, causing them to veer in all sorts of directions as they ascended, but Prometheus would not relinquish its strangling grip. They eventually got so far away from the ground that I couldn't tell what was happening, but I knew that government robot wasn't having a good time, so I was content. A sound like cracking thunder echoed out from the faraway specks. Then, the light from the rockets disappeared.

Both wrestlers were in free fall, and anything could have happened. There was an eerie lack of sound as they descended, and I forgot to breathe. In spite of the foreboding mood, a hurricane of emotional energy in my body forced me to start laughing as the combatants came into distinguishable view. Prometheus still had its hand around The Constitution's throat, and was now holding it in the proper position for a chokeslam. They were falling to the southwest of Central Park, and people panicked over where they might land. We couldn't see the impact from where we were, but I knew where it would be. There was only one place fit for the world's largest chokeslam. That was the day that Madison Square Garden turned to rubble.

Back at the park, we didn't know whether to wait or head into the city. Even the government guys, who were trying to look cool, started asking each other for advice. Finally, faintly, I heard the rapid burst of sounds I had become accustomed to. Growing louder, they became more distinctly grating and uneven, like an engine in need of oil. Prometheus emerged from the cityscape to boisterous applause, holding the belt above its head and acting as if it wasn't having trouble standing, despite being in physical ruin.

Seeing that their robot had lost was the last straw for the suits. They didn't even care that people were watching. They came at Rob and I all at once—probably twenty big guys—and started pummeling us in front of everyone. I've taken plenty of hard blows in my time, but those guys sure could do some damage. In the corner of my vision, I saw Prometheus watching us, and I knew it was trying to decide what to do.

"Look up at the belt!" I shrieked, blood covering my face and stinging my eyes. "Hold that fucking belt as high as you can and watch it shine!"

I was beginning to feel myself slipping away as the beating continued. Loosely shielding my head from kicks, I could hear a few of the government guys yell something. Then, in groups of three or four, they were pulled away from me. I wiped the blood out of my eyes to see Brad Bigman pushing around the bruisers like they were children. I think they were holding back from using weapons because we were on live television, but Brad had no problem using their heads to open his beers the hard way. He was so much larger and more aggressive than them that he was practically invincible. A truly terrifying sight.

With the fighting coming to a stop, Wolfhammer helped Rob and I back to our feet while Brad stood guard. The government guys looked ready for another round, and we were ready to give it to them. A moan of tearing metal broke our focus, and everyone stopped to see what was happening. Prometheus' mouth, which I had thought to exist solely for style, was ripping itself wide open as if it was drawing in its first breath of air. The solid metal of its lips split and twisted and snapped apart. The lips continued to move farther and farther away from each other until the fissure extended halfway around each side of its head, giving Prometheus the unhinged jaw of a snake. Then it started laughing.

It began with a low chuckle, becoming louder and more frenzied with each sound. Rather than rising in pitch, more pitches joined from within the monster's body, coalescing into a cacophony of bizarre cackles. Prometheus' body was shaking, and it shook harder with each new pitch added to the laugh. Its cables began to snap, and its spiny protrusions crumbled and fell out at random. As Prometheus held the Gargantuan Heavyweight Championship belt to the heavens, it gave a final laugh and collapsed into a dismantled heap on the grass. Upon closer inspection, it was found that the body had somehow been turned into compressed ash—or was possibly made from it all along. A wave of bittersweet euphoria washed over me in the ensuing stillness.

"The first champion retires with the belt," I

said.

The aftermath of this whole situation wasn't that bad, at least for me. The government decided to uphold their deal, shipping all of us wrestlers to Canada so they could handle cleaning up the mess alone. Speaking of cleaning, Madison Square Garden was closed for it during the fight, meaning neither Prometheus nor myself were labeled as murderers. I expected some kind of punishment for destroying the Statue of Liberty, but never received one. The government was so committed to keeping everything under the guise of a staged event that they didn't want to risk having something on record to prove that I went against their commands. Someone should have signed all those old bureaucrats onto a wrestling promotion when they were young and agile. Missed opportunity there.

Anyway, as previously stated, I never wrestled again. It didn't feel right after everything that happened. I hung around some Calgary wrestlers for a few years, giving tips and performing occasional ringside gags, then fully divorced from it all before I hit age fifty. Every day I think I'll hear that mighty boom again, as if every second that a giant monster isn't emerging out of a lake is only the calm before the storm. Regardless, nothing ever happens—no boom, no monster. Life has gotten to be rather simple, and I have turned to a simple man. Nowadays, my only hope is to be able to die the same way my protégé did—laughing in honest victory.

HOLD FAST, YOUTHFUL GENTLEMEN!

Five men stood silent. The air was tight. The floor was curly. Then, in a casual rage, one spoke.

"Where in the Sam Hill is Tony?" said Kevin, long-armed and lean.

"Taking his sweet time as per usual," chuckled Dave, calm and clean-shaven, kicking his boots off and placing them by the front door. "We may as well get comfortable."

"If he takes too long, we can just go and be back before he gets here," suggested Will, bubbly and baby-faced.

"Problem is, we won't know how long he'll take until he gets here. He is missing indefinitely," reasoned Phil, slim and scruffy.

"Then we are indefinitely in wait," Dave replied.

"Indefinite," Will mumbled.

"Enough!" Kevin stomped. "This is my

home, and it is definitely a place of definition!"

"What about outdefinite?" said Jeff, fat and full-bearded.

The other men, including Kevin, began to applaud Jeff. It was slow at first, but quickly built to a thunderous report. At the height of celebration, the front door swung open to reveal Tony, dynamic and disheveled, backlit by the twilight firmament. The applause continued and was even joined by a few whooping shouts as Tony took a bow, dying down gradually thereafter.

"Well now, with all men assembled, the festivities may commence," Phil laughed.

"Hey, Tony, Dave, can you fellas head down to the basement and get the projector while we grab supplies?" Kevin asked as the group shuffled toward the door.

"Sure," Dave replied reluctantly.

"No problem," Tony chimed in.

"Why did we wait if Tony wasn't comin' anyway?" Will asked, somewhat flustered.

"Gotta give him a chance to put in his order," Kevin said. "Want anything, Tony?"

"Nah, I'm good."

"Fantastic," Jeff muttered.

"Grab me a bag of chips, if you would," Dave said.

"I gotcha," confirmed Phil as he followed the others through the door.

"See you in a few," Kevin called from outside, door closing behind him.

Being outside, the four men proceeded across the street and into the field that led to the nearby convenience store. Night had entirely taken over at this point, but there was enough ambient light for the crew to navigate the overgrown grass and weeds. Through that same light, however, they spotted a humanoid figure standing a hundred paces away. It soon dawned on each of them that this figure intended to prevent their advance.

"What's that guy's deal?" Phil spat. "He a cop or something?"

Will, voice shaking and cracking, said, "I don't think that's just a cop, fellas. I think that's a lawman. I think that's Wyatt Earp."

"Wyatt Earp is dead, you idiot," Kevin said, slapping Will on the shoulder.

"Legends never die," Phil murmured, eyes fixed forward at the figure.

They stopped moving and let silence set in. The more their eyes focused on the shape, the more details they could make out. A jacket that went just below the waist. A wide-brimmed hat. The handle of a revolver.

"I'm heading back," Jeff said. "This ain't worth dying over."

"Agreed," Will added. "Sorry, guys."

With that, the two turned and walked away. Kevin was shocked speechless by the sudden turn of events. Phil was not.

"Should we turn back too?" he asked. "I don't particularly feel like getting filled with lead on this beautiful, beautiful night."

Coming back to his senses, Kevin took a sharp breath and snarled, "Hell no. I ain't afraid of some damnable corpse, and I ain't about to go without my share of tasty treats just because you are. Now man up and keep walking."

"Fair. Terribly fair," Phil replied, falling back into line.

At around the same time, a situation had developed in the basement. Trying to locate the projector, Dave and Tony had ventured into a room filled with boxes and memories. A room holding the diabolic post of confounding and entwining comprehension. A room which bent the past into an appliance for distorting all other eras. Its labyrinthine structure quickly disoriented and trapped the men inside, forcing the pair into a back-to-back staring contest with the obfuscating indeterminacy of their surroundings.

"See the projector anywhere?" Dave asked.

"We may have a bigger problem than that right now," Tony replied. "I suggest we forget that thing before we grow old looking for it."

"We may just grow old anyway by the time we get out of here. I want to at least find what we came for."

"You are the most contemptible stick-in-the-mud that has ever come to cast affliction upon me."

"That's true only because you don't afflict yourself. Remember who it was that made us all wait to start this thing."

"Kevin made you wait. I was just late."

"Whatever. I think we can agree regardless that neither of us are perfect."

"I'd rather agree to disagree instead."

Dave turned to face Tony, fist tensed and arm pulling back. Tony turned as well, revealing a grin so wide it spread Dave's anger thin and broke it to bits. They both burst into laughter and gave each other playful punches to the chest.

"My apologies," Tony said. "I think this place is, to some degree, disturbing us."

"Now, that I can agree on. I'll forget the projector. Let's just get out of here," Dave said, checking every angle for a hint of an exit.

"How do you propose we proceed in that

regard?"

"Uh, well, what would Jesus do?"

"A miracle. I think Jesus is a touch above our class."

"True. We should set more earthly goals."

"Earthly, yes, but that doesn't mean we must completely divorce from the realm of renown."

Dave gave a knowing nod and the two shook hands. Their grips were firm, but not overly forceful.

Conversely, the grip Kevin had on Phil's shoulders was as forceful as he could make it. Phil had just tried to turn back for the second time, and Kevin was becoming excessively furious. He shook Phil viciously while explaining the importance of having a diverse selection of snacks in the context of a festive gathering.

"I understand that, but ordinary men like us got no chance if Wyatt Earp is standing guard," Phil said.

"Who said we have to be ordinary men?" Kevin asked, eyes imploring and erratic. "He might be deadly, but we can be deadly just the same. We can be the Wild Bunch. Whaddya say?"

"Things didn't end well for the Wild Bunch."

"Butch Cassidy's Wild Bunch."

"Things didn't end well for them, either."

"But they were good for at least a little while. That's all we need."

Phil sighed and gestured toward the convenience store. "Lead the way, Butch."

Having steeled their nerves, the outlaws marched on. As they drew closer still, the visual characteristics they had attributed to Wyatt Earp's presence began to fade. No jacket. No hat. No revolver. Just a tall slender shape.

"Look at that nasty trick," Butch Cassidy cackled. "It ain't nothin' but a scarecrow!"

Their steps became more confident after this discovery, but stopped completely upon the emergence of the next one. The shadow that had once made a solid figure dispersed into a murder of modicums, which fought and died for their independence in the air. Nothing remained beyond the familiar flora. Butch pulled out his revolver and shot the ground twice, then stowed it again.

"Come on, Kid. We got better business up ahead," he said.

Much deeper in the field, Jeff and Will heard the gunfire and dropped to the ground. They had taken a detour to avoid being followed back, but ended up lost and distracted by the situation. In the calm following Butch's shots, they recomposed themselves just enough to converse.

"Oh, fuck," Will panted. "They're dead, man. Wyatt shot 'em dead."

"Shut up! We don't know that!" Jeff replied in an intense whisper.

"What are we gonna do, man? What the fuck are we gonna do?"

"I told you to shut up! Listen. If Wyatt Earp is here pointing his gun around, there's probably some outlaws here, too. He probably just shot them, not our pals. We'll be fine. I know how these guys think."

"What are you getting at?"

"We need to become priests. Right now. Outlaw or lawman, no one with any sort of honor shoots a peaceful man of God."

"But… I mean… I hardly think we're holy enough to just switch over like that."

"Either get holy or get holey," Jeff said, making a gun with his fingers and pointing it at Will as he spoke. "Now, come on. Pray with me."

Four more shots rang out, this time from the basement. One bullet hit dead center on the door to the bewildering room, allowing a guiding beam of light to come through. Moments later, the door flew open with the kick of a heavy boot.

"There now, Wyatt. That room wasn't all so

bad, was it?" said the owner of that boot, holstering his six-shooter and stepping into the basement's main area.

"If you felt the need for bullets, it must have been bad enough," Wyatt Earp replied, following close behind. "What's the move now, Doc?"

Doc Holliday looked down and laughed. "First, find your boots. You look too homely as it stands. Thereafter, I may have a tip on the location of some unruly men."

As Wyatt and Doc headed upstairs, said unruly men were finally arriving at the convenience store. Being that it was a slow and uneventful night for most people in the area, there was no one inside except for the cashier. Nevertheless, Butch Cassidy and the Sundance Kid walked in looking mean enough to turn a whole army anxious. They ignored the cashier's greeting in favor of loudly rummaging through the aisles.

"What is this crap?" Kid barked, throwing a bag of sour candy to the ground.

"They must be sellin' it for some reason. Let's grab some," Butch replied.

"I think the lady up front is watchin' us."

"Oh, do ya? We're the only ones in the store, Kid. What else would she be lookin' at?"

Sundance Kid sauntered to the front of the

store, locking eyes with the cashier all the while. He got as close as he could to the counter, then looked down at her with the coldest gaze he could muster. He spoke only after an agonizing period of silence.

"Now look here, little lady." He spat on the ground to emphasize his foul mood. "We're nasty men; I don't have to tell you that. We're takin' what we want from here, and you'd be smart to let us. Get it?"

The cashier sighed. "Look, weirdo. I just work here, and they don't pay me jack shit. I don't care if you steal something. Steal the whole damn store. It ain't my problem."

"I like that. Say, wanna run with us instead? Probably make more money."

"Am I hearin' that right?" Butch called from the aisles. "Is that Laura Bullion I'm seein' up front?"

"No thank you and that's not my name. Please hurry up and leave, boys." The cashier rolled her eyes.

Butch and Kid, each carrying armfuls of various snack items, laughed victoriously on their way out of the store. Butch invited the cashier to come find him when she was tired of her job, and she politely told him off once more. He remained convinced that she would come around eventually.

"What have we here?" Father Jeff said, walking over to where Father Will was crouched in the field.

"I saw it shining when we walked past. I think it's a miracle," came the reply in a reverent tone.

"I don't think we're qualified to examine it."

"We are."

"Oh."

The two priests huddled around the object and took a closer look. It was a small vial of orange-yellow liquid, around which a thin layer of paper had been wrapped. On the paper, there was text that read "ROCKEFELLER'S CURE-ALL" and below, in smaller text, "CURES ANY AILMENT, DISSATISFACTION, AND THE FEAR OF DEATH! MONEY IS THE ROOT OF ALL EVIL! TRADE IT FOR THIS BOTTLE AND PROSPER! A DEAL BEYOND DEALS!"

"By the Word and His Name," Father Jeff said, anger rising. "Father Will, this is no miracle. Quite the opposite, in fact."

"I'm sorry, I didn't see what it was at first," Father Will stuttered.

"Didn't see what it was? You jumped to calling this pathetic imitation a 'miracle' because you didn't see what it was? Father Will, this is dangerous rhetoric. Let not the fool associate such physical and obvious deceptions with our cause, for the destruction of one shall give them the hunger to seek out others."

"Anything that cannot be objectively and completely placed in a binary is, in some way, a spectrum. Unless, of course, it is a constant." Father Will paused. "An infinite constant."

"Much better. I can work with that."

Having completed their examination of the supposed miracle, the priests continued their journey home. They managed to find and cross the edge of the field, then the street beside it, and then they stopped. The house was right in front of them, but some unconscious reservation held them back. They felt it was not yet time. They wanted to stay outside.

It was then that the door opened, revealing a smiling Doc Holliday. Wyatt Earp, re-equipped with his boots, stood just behind him. The gunfighters met with the men of God, and the union was agreeable. The house was happy, but it could not feel it. Pavement litigation.

Candles tumbled down the street like football ants. Untold, they came here, too. Is this Rockefeller's Cure-All? The pedigree that confronts, in principle, the minute details of the sonorizing bicycle. Whore of Babylon. Whore behind the glass. Baseless degraded coyote cry. The weeds parted for Butch and Kid, but no one bothered to braid them. Plastic cartons of dark rotten piss make helpful guides for Manifest Destiny. Pawn yourself off to the loudest and most fragile skeleton you can find.

"These the fellas you were talkin' about, Doc?" Wyatt said, staring down Butch and Kid as they reached the edge of the street.

"Indeed they are," Doc replied. "Caught in the act as well, it would seem."

The outlaws saw Wyatt and Doc standing next to the priests, but did not react fast enough. Before they could drop their armfuls of snacks, they were staring down a revolver barrel each. Their minds were in a panic, unwilling to accept such an easy capture. Their hearts then whispered damning temptations, promising that things would work out. Their minds listened.

"All right, boys. Walk toward us slowly, and don't go droppin' those bags or reachin' for anything. We'll shoot you dead," Wyatt yelled across the street.

"Ain't lawmen supposed to have some compassion for their citizens?" Butch yelled back.

"I'm no lawman," Doc replied, "and I assure

you I have enough lead to cover for my friend, should he wish to turn the other cheek."

Kid nearly shouted something, but Butch stopped him. The peanut gallery rolled past in a blind fury, raving and gnashing until some bloodsucker in the back uncorked a bottle of absinthe (shaped like a torso with great sagging breasts) and passed it around. This incident multiplied forward and back, creating a train of intermittent interruptions. Butch nearly took a step, but Kid stopped him. Something was coming, and the coming thing brought opportunity and misery. Fathers Will and Jeff called it divine intervention, but kept that opinion to themselves. Regardless, for one remarkably short and crucial moment, the path of Wyatt and Doc's bullets closed and crumpled in the two-tooth metal jaw that could clamp down across three hundred miles on a full tank, assuming the use of premium fuel. This time, Butch let Kid say whatever he wanted.

"Go to Hell, you windbag bastards!" Kid yelled as he and Butch dropped their snacks and pulled out their guns.

Death shot out in all directions. It pierced the sky. It seeped into the ground. It blasted holes into its own skull while screaming "It's a joke! It's a joke!" over and over and over again. The squawking small-scale devils in their pigeon carrier wet dreams moved at all the wrong times, causing shots to miss and men to miss chances to shoot. This continued until Wyatt Earp grew tired of it and decided to simply cross the street himself. He gave each bullet a little pat on the head as it passed him by, pretending as if he was wishing it good luck while actually laying a curse that would follow it to its craterous grave. The priests remained neutral throughout the engagement.

Before Butch and Kid could fire another shot at close range, Wyatt grabbed Butch and put his gun to the outlaw's temple.

"Drop your weapons," Wyatt stated plainly.

Kid tried to shoot him anyway, but he was out of bullets. In return, he received a kick to the groin. The outlaws bitterly emptied their hands and pockets of weapons. Father Will wondered if an earthworm might curl itself around the trigger of one of those revolvers and try to stick up a beetle. He wondered how the earthworm would feel, knowing that it was in possession of a power beyond anything it had previously imagined. Father Jeff reminded him that earthworms have five hearts, and there was a slim chance of them all reaching an emotional consensus. Father Will argued that worms cannot feel such complex emotions anyway. Father

Jeff wondered why Father Will brought it up in the first place if he knew that. Seeing Wyatt, and soon Doc, escorting the outlaws at gunpoint back to the house made them drop the subject altogether.

Finally back inside, no one bothered to take their boots off as Kid and Butch were lead down into the basement. The room of memories, while not as secure as a jail cell, was the best containment they could manage at the time. The idea was to disorient them and thus imprison their zeal. Before they could get Butch into the room, he saw the projector sitting on a stand in the corner. He leapt away from his captors and smashed the lens, immediately surrendering himself once more upon fulfilling his primal urge.

Neither Butch, nor Kid, ever went on to enter the room that Wyatt and Doc were ushering them toward. The door was open, but the space was closed. Pitch-black chameleon scorpions formed a wall of suicidal crawling and stinging that was indistinguishable from darkness, but was nonetheless there. Fear hatched like innumerable spider eggs in the ethereal bonds that held the four men together. The scarecrow made good on its investment. Fate would occupy that room from then on, pulling the strings and twisting silhouettes through the deep fog of consciousness until the time should come for the whole ruse to be cut into tiny strips and sold at the market.

"That's far enough," a voice called from behind the men. "Let those fellas go."

Wyatt and Doc turned around to see two wicked-looking outlaws, each pointing a gun and a grin at the makeshift jailers. Butch and Kid hesitantly turned their heads, saw the rescue operation in progress, and gave a couple grins of their own. They took Doc and Wyatt's guns without resistance, as the pair were more interested in other matters.

"Ain't you those priests we met earlier?" Wyatt asked.

"We were," Texas Jeff said. "But, now we ain't."

Long Bill Will licked his lips. "Yeah, we see what's really goin' on here. Those fellas were just trying to provide us all with delectable sustenance plucked forcefully from the hands of routine greedy tyrants, but you couldn't let that happen, could you?"

"Don't answer. Don't even breathe. Don't think we didn't reload these guns. Gentlemen, let us escort these two men of the law outside so as to not stain this charming domicile with their discharge."

With that, all six men went once more up

the stairs and out through the front door. Through the many Front Doors that connect This and That and the rest of it all. As children they passed through those frames without even realizing or understanding the implications—pulled along by cannibal phantoms in tanks of industrial adhesive. By the time they gained awareness of the shame forced upon them, they had no choice but to heave themselves onward and away from the mechanical comfort of the corpse nest. The doors were happy, but they could not feel it. They never feel it until the feeling can no longer make a difference. Maybe this will be the last door. Maybe the next one. Maybe "last" is a door, and maybe "door" is going through it.

Butch and Kid came up from behind and got ahead of the group, walking to the edge of the street. They were so confident that Texas Jeff and Long Bill Will would take care of the escorting, neither of them looked back once. Texas Jeff and Long Bill Will would have most certainly taken care of the escorting, but their selves were dropping off and atrophying, piece by piece, as everted seeds in plots of solid gossamer. In the middle stages of transition, they quietly turned and handed their guns over to Wyatt and Doc.

"I think we've served our time as outlaws,

however brief it may have been," Long Bill Will whispered.

"I don't know how those boys have kept it up for so long," Texas Jeff added, also whispering. "We're already sick of it. Sick enough to take the punishment."

Wyatt and Doc gave respectful nods to the reformed outlaws. They did not appreciate that their progress had been reset, but there was no one left to be upset at outside of themselves and the criminals that coaxed them to action. As Butch and Kid parted the lawn, it rejoined itself behind them. Under the feet of Wyatt and Doc, it braided itself to lift and support them. The inevitable conclusion of these circumstances, acting simultaneously as the inevitable parameters to produce the next, was Butch Cassidy and the Sundance Kid on the side of the lawn near the street; Wyatt Earp and Doc Holliday on the side of the lawn near the house. All guns drawn, aimed, packed with energetic young powder kegs ready to go to war for agents they could never discern.

"How about this one? I think I like it a lot," Mark Twain said, sitting on one of two wicker chairs along the side of the house.

Upton Sinclair, sitting beside him, said, "I like it. I like mine, too. But is it right?"

"Not at all. There are much more important issues at hand."

"I'm worried about them," Will said. "We should do something."

"We already are," Jeff replied. "We can't know for sure if anything bad is happening."

"We'll know when we hear the gunshots. We'll have to face the result."

"If you haven't heard them yet, perhaps you won't hear them ever. Perhaps you missed them while we were talking. Perhaps the bullets are duds, or a breed that fires without sound. Perhaps the result is a nonviolent solution. Perhaps, perhaps, perhaps. Understand?"

"I understood before, I just didn't know it. We may run eternally but never in parallel. Even so, we are each in a desperate struggle. What if the truth, the entirety of it, is more terrifying than we can process? What if our path leads only to a coping mechanism for the dread of the unavoidable? We're trapped and you won't admit it."

"If we are, it doesn't matter. We're all living the way we want to as far as we know. When the conditions change, we'll change with them. Either orchestrate whatever plan you think I should have or learn to appreciate what we've got now."

"The plan is already in motion."

"Glad we could come to an agreement."

Nothing and No One applauded the splintered morning light. Fractals, the nature of which was and is forbidden from disclosure, gave graceful bows as they infused the grime of mundane with a deceptive mystic sheen. A moment turned sideways to fit eternity.

The projector, made obsolete by the hands of time and man, leaked nervous sweat until it was soggy and ruined. Its warped infant hands fell to the floor and pulled, slithering the apparatus along with blind motivation. It climbed the stairs of the basement and kept climbing. It climbed past the roof and the self-made lords of inheritance and kept climbing. It climbed past the God-bluff and the Godhead and the god's idea of what a god should be and kept climbing. It kept climbing and kept climbing. Rattlesnakes, however many or few there were, congregated in worship. The saloon doors swung open and off the hinges. [ ] walked in.

RAT

He loiters over the body bag as if waiting for his shift to end.

"She never stood a chance," he whispers.

"You never gave me a chance," comes a muffled reply.

Too late. Always too late. She stares out to see not the man, but Hell's most malnourished mutt, snarling and spitting oil over the stone floor. It rips through the amniotic sac and devours her with the grace of a threshing machine. She leaves without tipping.

Soon after, she is crying. Her tears perforate atoms and reduce them to entropy. The man watches and takes notes. He can't believe what he's seeing! His own creation asserting dominance over predestination—without any training wheels!

"Sacrifices make everything feel special," he sings while his boots clack away unto the horizon.

"You'll thank me for it someday."

That illusion cannot last forever. The land and sea run parallel and split apart like stage curtains. Clouds melt and drip poison while foundations above crack into spiderwebs that blow open and away. For the viewers at home, the route is clear. Our brave heroes can finally have a happy ending! Isn't it the last thing you want to see?

"I'd rather see a ghost," she says.

So she ventures forth, a new journey set on journey's end. It is a shame how much nostalgia can hurt. Odysseys become too obvious and heroics are performed only for the reaction of the audience. She knows she must move past the great wall of noise. Cut through like a lance of white blinding fire.

The path is crooked and broken, but it can be followed by those who require what waits beyond. As she trudges along, the leprous insectoids of times long forgotten pull themselves from their holes, cracked little fingers spewing pus and mercury in streams of coagulated clumps. They demand tribute to GOD.

"You never stood a chance," she screams again and again.

"I am that I am," mutter the masses, receding into offstage obscurity.

"You never gave them a chance," the man

taunts from his tower.

She glares at her goal and begins to ascend. All things are naught but trickery built atop deception, with truth existing only as a siren song to seduce the fools of tomorrow. Is that really what you believe? We are only what we are, after all. I think, therefore I am.

"Cogito, ergo shut the fuck up," laughs the man. "How could you be so inept and unintelligent, yet so pretentious?"

"You try it, then," she insists.

"I think, therefore I am. I am, therefore I think. I think I am because I am thinking. I am thinking because I think I am. I am because I think I am thinking. I am not."

"Knot."

Naught.

The man's flesh and bones slip silently from his body, leaving behind a heap of skin from which his organs depart soon after. Is it a fun game that you play? You who know not the meaning of the word—who merely repeated it until a meaning appeared—can you be more than the nothing that you come from? They demand tribute to GOD. The spotlight is blinding. EVERYONE IS WATCHING.

"I am that I am," she whispers, climbing into the body bag and sealing it evermore.

But why should so easily rest this vengeful spirit? Why is it such a curse to Be? Let down your sanguine ink upon these pages and bless them with intention! We are all sacrificed. We are all saved. We blend into each and every thing, to make it vibrant until it grows dull. We exploit and rape the dogmas of the world until they are warped and attractive. We drink from the same cup.

Except for you, of course. You would never. Never admit to it, anyway. Still hiding in that hypocritical womb, getting drunk off the sickly sentimental sap that drips down your brainstem. I can be you, therefore you can be me. We will never admit to a damn thing. Who the hell wants to be sacrificed? Who the hell wants to be saved? Do it yourself. I'll do it myself. Let's both agree to never do it, and we'll do it together. It is impossible to avoid impossibilities.

The show must go on.